THE DSA SEASON ONE, BOOK FOUR

SPECTRAL ADVOCATE

Also by Lou Paduano

The Greystone Saga

Signs of Portents
Tales from Portents
The Medusa Coin
Pathways in the Dark
A Circle of Shadows

Greystone-in-Training

Hammer and Anvil

The DSA

Season One
The Clearing
Promethean
The Bridge

THE DSA SEASON ONE, BOOK FOUR

SPECTRAL ADVOCATE

Lou Paduano

Eleven Ten Publishing LLC

GRAND ISLAND, NEW YORK

Eleven Ten Publishing LLC
282 Fareway Lane
Grand Island, NY 14072

Publisher's note: This is a work of fiction. Names, characters, places, and incidents either are the product of the author's imagination or are used fictitiously. Any resemblance to actual events, locales, or persons, living or dead, is entirely coincidental.

Printed in the United States of America
Edited by JD Book Services.
Cover art design by MiblArt

First edition published 2020

Library of Congress Cataloguing in Publication Data
Paduano, Lou
Spectral Advocate / Lou Paduano

LCCN: 2020900029
ISBN-13: 978-1-944965-24-2 (paperback)
ISBN-13: 978-1-944965-23-5 (eBook)

For Brad Korbesmeyer
A remarkable teacher and an even better friend.

CHAPTER ONE

The young boy woke with a start and raced for the door. The floor creaked and moaned with his footfalls as the terror of the dream tracked his every movement. Opening the door a crack, he saw a stream of light from the reading lamp in his parents' room.

His father read the newspaper, always a day behind thanks to a tireless work schedule. His hair was dotted gray at the temples, receding inch by inch every year. A mark of survival, he joked whenever the comment flew from neighbors and friends. No one understood his life—*their* lives. Not when the doors closed and the locks were in place.

At the sound of the pattering steps, the middle-aged man wearing horn-rimmed glasses sighed and closed the paper. The shadow of the boy ran in the slit of the doorway.

"Bad dream again?" he grumbled, his voice a whisper to keep his wife from waking. The man staggered from his bed, slippers in place to protect his feet from the cold of the hardwood floors. It also created a buffer from more noise in the room. She needed her sleep. Another illness kept her bedridden. He respected her need just as she had his own over the years.

The door opened and the man, tall and proud, peered down on the boy. His father was clean-cut and lean, a hidden physicality he attempted to pass along to his waif of a son. The boy's head nodded, the terror hovering in his eyes.

"Yes."

His father guided him back to his room and closed the door behind him. "Come on."

The boy ran back to the bed and jumped in. He pulled the

covers up to his head and settled on the pillow. His father joined him along the edge, following his movements with exacting eyes. It was the same cold stare he carried all day, every day.

"What was it this time?" he asked the child, hidden under the rocket-ship sheets.

"Ghosts," the boy mumbled, ashamed and scared to give the nightmare voice. "They came through the window and I tried to run, but the monster in the closet stopped me and I—"

"Hey," his father stopped him, then lowered his voice. "Hey, now. You know what I'm going to say, don't you?"

"Yeah," his son groaned. "Monsters aren't real. Ghosts don't exist."

"Exactly."

The same cop-out. The nightmares *felt* real. They took hold and never stopped, trailing his every thought, marking every shadow in the room despite the *Superman* nightlight his mother had bought him for his birthday.

"But, Dad—"

"No. No more of that," his father said in a sharp tone. Deep eyes in the dark pierced the young man and silenced the argument before it could occur. There was no point. His father was right, always and completely, no matter the subject. "Listen to me, kiddo. I'm a cop. I know what I'm talking about."

"This isn't—"

"Ben," his father said. "I've seen monsters, and they don't have sharp claws and fangs. They also don't hang out in closets, especially this one. And ghosts? Ben, it's time to put away those thoughts. The world doesn't work on wonder and imagination, but through hard work and determination. You can be so much more. You just have to stop being afraid."

"I'm not like you," Ben replied, arms across his chest and lips in a pout. "I don't know how to be strong like you."

"You'll figure it out, Ben. I promise you that." His father left the comfort of the bed and finished tucking him under the sheets. "I'll be there to help you become the man I know you can be. The man I *hope* you'll be."

"You think I can?" his son said, his eyes heavy and the pillow welcoming him. "I can be like you someday?"

"You'll be better than me. I promise." His father ran his hand through Ben's hair and smiled—a rare treat, one always hidden away behind responsibility and duty. "Now I need you to get some sleep and remember what I said."

"Right," the boy said with a yawn. "Ghosts aren't real, and monsters don't exist."

His father nodded, heading for the door. His words were soft and lost on the wind as Ben Riley drifted off to sleep. "Not here, kiddo. Not while I'm around."

CHAPTER TWO

Sleep shunned Ben. It taunted him, his eyes heavy from the late hour. Every chance he had, every opportunity to rest, sent his mind reeling. He beat against his pillow, and he screamed into the sheets, begging for a moment's peace from the long night.

Still, rest eluded him — too many questions plagued Ben, too much second-guessing followed by thirds and fourths like an all-you-can-eat buffet of doubt and recriminations. All were centered on a single event, one he hadn't taken part in, yet continued to pay for because of his recruitment to the mysterious covert agency known as the DSA.

The death of Jacob Grissom.

He left the comfort of his bed in defeat. The file remained squarely on the desk residing in his spare room. He clicked on the small lamp on the thin tabletop. The file beamed under the spotlight, burning a hole in his mind and begging him for answers.

None came. What could he think? When he read the pages, the operation detailed the man's fall so clearly from the perspectives of all involved that only one conclusion could be made: Susan Metcalf had let the man die.

The decision was hers, the choice to leave him behind when the field team had begged for a second chance to save their colleague and friend. She stopped them — the operation had been a success. One man paid the price to save hundreds, possibly thousands from Blake's virus hitting the streets.

To the rest of the Department of Special Assignments, the cost was too great, as well as unnecessary. Greg Sullivan, the newly installed deputy director, believed it to be the case, going one step further even to call Metcalf a murderer. He claimed that her actions were from jealousy, of a fear of losing her position to Grissom. His death had protected her livelihood.

Ben opened the window to the apartment, the frigid air shocking him awake. He grabbed his button-down shirt, casually discarded to the floor during his late-night reading, and slipped it on. The thin fabric did little to warm him in the winter chill ripping through the seventh-floor apartment.

Could it have been true? Was Metcalf capable of premeditated murder, sending Grissom to his death with an unnecessary secondary objective? Had she sabotaged the operation from the start, alerting Blake to their presence before the team had made their move?

Sullivan believed it to be true. His own motivations, however, were suspect. He wanted Metcalf gone, removed from the DSA. He had something to gain by drawing Ben to his side, but how much of the tale was true? Why did Ben still doubt any of his accusations considering what he'd spent the night reading?

Yet doubts remained. Metcalf had recruited Ben, saved him from a jail sentence. The world had buried him in the dark yet she'd offered a fresh start—a second chance to make something of his life.

Why him? He assumed she'd followed his case and recognized something in him. Now that he knew she had been watching him for years, that assumption rang false. She had followed his career, operatives tracking his every move at times. Why? How far did her involvement go? Was she behind the circumstances of his setup? Had she coerced Horace Waters into ruining his career, exiling him from his home and his friends?

"Dammit!"

Ben rubbed his eyes, resting along the frame of the open window. Nothing made sense. Every thought blurred, bleeding colors along a canvas of shadow. Sullivan or Metcalf? Who was right? Who was wrong?

Did Ben have a choice in the matter?

Sullivan made it clear he didn't. The threat layered beneath his subtle manipulations during their impromptu meeting the previous day spoke to the lack of options for Ben. He could either side with Sullivan and spy on Metcalf's every move, or enjoy a prison sentence.

Prison wasn't sounding so bad anymore.

Maybe he deserved the sentence after all this time. He had never been the best cop, never lived up to the potential his father demanded. When Waters had framed him, when he'd faced a jury of his peers, perhaps they had seen the truth better than he ever could.

A scream cut across the gap outside. Ben's bloodshot eyes snapped awake, scanning the adjacent corridors of the Edgemont Apartment building. One floor up, directly overlooking his unit, was an open window. A shadow raced against the glass, and lights flickered in a dim glow.

Ben's brow creased and he pushed away from the sill. It wasn't his concern. No, only the file resting on his desk mattered—and the lack of options left to him on both sides of the argument.

He could leave Bethesda and the DSA. Run and never look back. It was a chance to start again, this time making every decision on his own. He could live the life he had always wanted—not that he knew what that might be. Not that he'd ever known what he wanted in life. He had spent so long fighting against the darkness of his father's incredibly long shadow that Ben had never had the chance to figure out his own path. Maybe it was time to start.

The scream returned, loud and shrill. Pained agony stretched the gap from the single open window across the way. Ben raced from the desk to the sill. What the hell was he thinking? Was he so far gone he could ignore a cry for help?

Never.

Ben pulled his shirt across his chest and blitzed for the living room. His badge sat on the partition separating the living room from the kitchen, and he slipped it into his pocket without pause. Then he grabbed his sidearm from the holster hanging on the mantel. The cartridge dislodged; there was a full complement ready and waiting. He slammed it back in place, then chambered a round.

Barefoot and cold while his over-sized pajama bottoms caught against the heels of his feet, Ben started for the door to his apartment. He yanked it from the frame for the shadows of the hall. Ben took a sharp breath, then raced into the darkness once more — hoping it wouldn't swallow him whole.

CHAPTER THREE

Thought escaped him. Seconds ticked by though it felt like an eternity. The world silenced around him. Ben was grateful for the reprieve, content to have something to do instead of mull over his options, despite the growing weariness in his bones.

The flight of stairs to the eighth floor of the Edgemont faded behind him. His bare feet slid along the stained carpet of the corridor. Dim lights ran along the center of the ceiling. Ben blinked rapidly, resisting the heaviness of his eyes. The cold metal of the Ruger sent a chill along his arm. He held the weapon tight to his side. Despite the emptiness of the hall, Ben took each step slower than the last. Each door remained closed and each shadow caught on his periphery was his own.

When a door opened to his left he nearly opened fire on instinct. An elderly woman with rollers in her hair and thick glasses staggered from her apartment. Her eyes thinned at the sight of him and his weapon. Never stopping, never backing away, the woman raised a frying pan at him, ready to swing.

Ben lowered the gun and tucked it in his waistband. He opened his badge for her, though her attention was elsewhere. Her gaze trailed down from his awkward smile to his bare chest.

"Great," Ben muttered, attempting to close his shirt. He continued down the hall. As he passed her, a needy paw pinched his ass. "Hey!"

The woman chuckled, the pan holstered under her arm. She licked her lips slowly, hand to the frame of her apartment. Her words were rapid mumbles, the language foreign and incomprehensible to the exhausted agent.

Ben nodded politely as he backed away from her creeping

hand. Before he could respond, a wrenching sound echoed down the corridor. Wood cracked, once then twice in quick succession, before shattering. When he turned back to the woman, her door was closed and the chain lock was sliding into place.

Swiping at his eyes, Ben rounded the corner for the far side of the building. The third door on the left was exposed. The heavy oak had been snapped at the lock. It hammered against the back wall, unable to make the return trip to the frame. Splinters were scattered inside the hall of the apartment and right outside. The intruder's footprints were clearly marked through the debris.

Hand to the door to keep it in place, Ben entered the apartment. His gun led the way. No more screams guided him. The aid was no longer necessary to track its origin point.

The domicile matched his own, reversed because of its location in the building. Just inside the entrance was a small hallway. Green carpeting ran throughout. The bathroom was tucked on the right and the door was open a crack. Ben edged the door back. He caught his reflection in the mirror.

I look like crap.

He cleared the room quickly, then wheeled down the hall for the rest of the apartment. Opposite the bathroom was the kitchen, which bled into the main living space of the two-bedroom unit.

Dishes were stacked in the sink, one plate, a coffee cup, silverware, and a wine glass. The wrapper of the microwave meal peeked from the lidless trash in the corner. It looked like a lonely night in, matching most of his when not in the field for the DSA.

A single occupant clearly lived there. Female, from what he could tell from the decorations. Candles sat along the counter. A bright pink sweatshirt hung over the lounger in the corner of the living room.

The place looked newly furnished, the couches factory fresh. *Someone new to the area? Their first apartment?*

Speculation fell behind the sound of heavy breathing in the living room. Away from the couches dotting the space on the left-hand side lay a woman along the carpet. She stared up at the ceiling. Gaping lips of ruby red and deep, recessed green eyes welcomed him to their emptiness. Thin, black locks of hair were scattered underneath her, spreading like a fan along the ground.

No wounds were visible, and no blood spread beneath her

along the recently installed carpet. At least not that Ben noticed. His focus was locked on the pair of hands pressing with all their might between her breasts.

A figure knelt close to her body. His wrinkled shirt and moppy brown hair obscured Ben's view of the victim.

"Don't move!" Ben shouted, awake to the situation at last. He raised his sidearm, maintaining a safe distance from the man looming over the deceased in the room. "Hands where I can see them!"

The man's arms fell limply to his sides, the heavy breathing from the act of supplying CPR to the dead woman slowly fading. He turned to face Ben, hands spread to show their emptiness.

"This looks kinda bad, doesn't it?"

CHAPTER FOUR

This is bad, isn't it?

Zac Modine leaned along the edge of the bed and ran his hand through his hair. His eyes refused to focus, and the shadows in the room were thick like tar—surrounding him in the unfamiliar space. The phone rattled in his hand, though he wasn't sure if it was nerves or exhaustion as he held it tight to his ear.

"No… Listen," he whispered into the phone. Water ran in the background and he tossed the comforter aside, then dangled his legs along the side of the mattress. "I'm the one who should be apologizing. It's been… it's been busy at work. I keep losing track of the time."

He covered the speaker and let out a long breath. His heart pounded in his ears. The clock beamed 5:23 in bright red letters. Each incessant tick condemned him for his betrayal of the woman on the other end of the call.

Her words were quiet and accepting—questioning, yet patient. More patient than he deserved, considering the sharpness of his own tone.

"You know I can't talk about work," he replied, sweaty fingers slipping from the cell phone speaker. "It's nothing, Claire. No, I know. I said I would, so I—"

The water turned off and he could hear the pitter-patter of footsteps from the door behind him. Humming from inside the bathroom boomed in his ears. He tucked the phone closer. His forehead was drenched.

"What?" His voice cracked at the question. He didn't hear her, couldn't make out the sound of her words. Each inflection caught in his thoughts, accusing him without saying a single thing.

"They're coming for dinner?" His in-laws. He hadn't made the time to see them in weeks, even though they lived five minutes away from Zac's small home outside the city. He hadn't made the time to see *anyone* other than those at work. The DSA acted both as a home and place of employment with each passing day. It still felt that way despite his questioning attitude and his growing doubts thanks to Metcalf's actions.

He loved his work. He loved... well, that was the question, wasn't it?

"I'll be there," he lied, wondering how long he had left on the call. There was a lack of movement beneath the frame of the bathroom door. "I'll talk to my boss about it."

Zac swiped at his forehead, trying to mop up the layers of sweat. He ran his hands through the sheets, twisted and unraveled at the corners of the bed. His mind flashed, lost to the night.

"Zac? Are you okay?" Claire's voice called to him, begged for him to return to the conversation. He heard someone else calling his name, repeating the word louder and louder. "Zac?"

"Huh?" he responded, blinking away the memory. "Did you say something?"

"I said I love you, goof," his wife declared.

"Yeah, I... Yeah..." Zac muttered. "I have to go, Claire. Tell Alex I... Right. When he gets up. I'll be home when I can."

The phone fell silent, dropped from his slick palm to the ground below. He had almost said it, the instinct taking over all common sense. *I love you too.* Such a simple phrase, one used daily over the course of their six years together. He had almost said it again, as if it was all the same, as if he hadn't changed everything in their dynamic.

As if his clothes were not lying in a pile at the side of someone else's bed.

What was I thinking? The clock continued to tick away the minutes loudly. He hadn't been home in two days. The call was as much routine as the phrase that repeated itself in the back of his mind. It was one he couldn't say, not without more regret—not without the guilt that came from staring at the pile of discarded clothes or his naked body reflected in the mirror.

Steps slid closer. A shadow slipped from the adjacent bathroom. Steam billowed against her ebony frame. She melded with the darkness and her soft flesh danced to the mattress like a cat. Hands ran along his back and over his shoulders, nails digging playfully into his skin.

Zac kicked at the phone to hide it under his clothing. He buried it as easily as his conversation with Claire so he could focus on the room for the first time since his companion left for the shower.

Morgan Dunleavy grinned devilishly behind him, her teeth beaming in the mirror. Her body was like a furnace against his back. It burned him to the core. He didn't move, letting it happen.

Her lips caressed his neck. She nibbled at his ear. "We still have some time."

He turned in surprise, meeting her kiss. Zac melted in her arms. "Morgan…"

"Shhh. Isn't this what you want?"

He had never expected this. When he'd assisted in reconnecting her with her family, ending her self-exile, Zac had never wanted anything in return. He had merely been looking out for a co-worker, as he would anyone in the agency, wasn't he?

No, Morgan was more than a colleague in his eyes and she recognized it in his actions. In her thank you, the kiss that took his breath away. And in her offer later that night.

He had meant to say no. He wanted to walk away, to be the dutiful husband and dedicated father. Instead, he had accepted the invitation to her place, where he'd gotten lost in her eyes, her hands, her body.

"Zac?" she asked, the question on her lips once more. "Isn't it?"

"Yes."

Her smile grew. She pulled him close and her heat swallowed him whole. He burned with her and for her all in one. He tried to resist, tried to fight the urge that had built since their time in Chicago.

She needed him, though, and he accepted the role. More than that, he felt the same. He joined her fully in the shadows of the bedroom, staring deep into her ravenous eyes. He couldn't help but accept her embrace.

CHAPTER FIVE

The man was slow to turn, hands shaking from being held over his head for an extended amount of time. Silence filled the space between them. Silence and an endless rush of information as Ben scanned the figure crouched beside the dead woman in the apartment.

His hair was overgrown and fell over his forehead in a thick chestnut-colored clump. He was young—mid to late twenties from the look of him—with pale skin as if he were stuck indoors most of the time. His eyes betrayed his youthful appearance, sky-blue in the center and old, holding more experience in them than Ben could ever imagine.

"I know how this looks."

Ben thought the exact same thing, his gun leveled on the kneeling man. He continued to survey the residence. The windows were locked, all except the one sending cold air from the spare bedroom. Clear sight lines made him aware the man with the wrinkled shirt and loosened tie was the only player in the place—the only possible killer.

"If I could just..." the man continued with a nervous smirk on his lips. His hand lowered for the breast pocket on his button-down shirt.

Ben took a step closer, the gun taking the lead. "I said don't move!"

The kneeling man froze in place. A cool resolve edged into each word. "You did. You definitely mentioned the no moving part. But just give me a second and I—"

The hand lowered once more, slower this time. Ben tugged at his lower lip with his teeth. "Keep your damn hand—"

"I didn't do this, and the sooner we move past this very tense moment, the sooner we can have a civilized conversation about it." The man's head tilted to the dead woman behind him. "Possibly one that's away from the deceased. That's your call, of course."

This was getting them nowhere, and both recognized the uncomfortable stand-off. Answers were needed. Ben nodded, using his sidearm to motion for the leather sofa positioned in front of the locked windows in the living room. The crouched man found his footing, then quietly shuffled over to the couch with hands visible above his head. He hesitated at the edge of the cushion. Liquid ran down the armrest to the floor. It was clear and thick, yet no sign of a glass was present in the room.

"Right there is fine," Ben insisted, patience wearing thin.

"Really?" The gun repeated the order and the young man sat on the couch, though he shuffled away from the goopy liquid on the cushion as much as possible.

The woman on the floor lay exposed for the first time since Ben entered the room. She wore tight shorts and a thin tank-top, not the typical attire considering the temperature outside. Ben glanced at the thermostat. It was set particularly high, yet the area surrounding her was nowhere near that warm. It was freezing, in fact.

Ben leaned close, an eye toward the sitting suspect on the other side of the room. The exhausted agent's fingers grazed the woman's neck and checked her vitals, to no avail. Whatever happened had come suddenly. There was no sign of a struggle—no visible cuts or bruises. Fear in her green eyes begged for answers.

"Who are you?" Ben stood, pacing the outskirts of the living space. The bedroom was empty, the sheets still made. Heat blasted thanks to the open window, rushing from the vents in the corners. It failed to penetrate the perimeter surrounding the deceased. *Why is it so cold here and only here?*

Ben's search brought him behind the couch to the bank of three windows. Clear liquid ran down from the sill. It looked like silicone and dripped on the carpet beneath. His full attention returned to the man on the couch, whose hand moved for the breast pocket again. "Don't even..."

The man shook his head, continuing for the pocket. Dipping

in with two fingers, he retrieved a small card and held it out in front of him. Ben paused opposite the coffee table dividing them.

"It's a business card. I had ten thousand printed, so I like to hand them out."

Ben snatched it from him and looked it over. Black bold letters blanketed the center of the card with the man's name and occupation.

CAVLIN COOPER
ATTORNEY AT LAW

The address didn't ring any bells for Ben, but he recognized the 518 area code to the phone number listed at the bottom of the card. An Albany, New York, number. The young man shuffled off the edge of the cushion, almost standing to point at the card.

"There's a typo in there," he said with a wince. "I always forget about that typo. Had a friend make them up. He doesn't like to talk about it. I asked him to spell check before finalizing the order. Twice, actually, mostly because he tends to tune you out unless you repeat yourself... I'm rambling now, aren't I?" He tried to smile, but stopped when he recognized Ben's vacant stare. He extended his hand. "Cal. Cal Cooper."

"Sit back down," Ben replied without moving.

Cal's hand fell away and he returned to the cushion. "Right."

"A lawyer?"

"Yeah," Cal said, clearing his throat. "Yes. That's right. And you are...? Some kind of late-night escort service that dabbles in security on the side? Just a guess."

Ben looked down—he'd forgotten about his exposed chest. He rolled his eyes, tucking the business card into his pajama pocket. He retrieved his badge and threw it to the suspect, letting him look it over while Ben buttoned up his shirt.

"Agent Benjamin Riley. DSA," Cal read stoically. He tossed the badge back to Ben's waiting hand. "DSA? Sounds made up."

Ben pointed to the dead woman in the middle of the room. "You know what this looks like, Cal Cooper the lawyer? Cause right now I don't see any sign of someone else in this room. There's also nothing out of place or missing to indicate a robbery gone wrong. Do you see where I'm going with this?"

Cal nodded, inching to the edge of the couch. "I do. But

Agent Winslow was—"

"I'm sorry?" Ben interrupted. His eyes widened with surprise. "Did you say Winslow? Abigail Winslow?"

"You knew her?"

"Not yet. I was supposed to, but..." Ben's reply faded at the sight of the woman lying on the carpet. Winslow had been the newest recruit for the field team of the DSA. He was supposed to meet her the previous morning before her tour of the warehouse facility that served as the department's base of operations. Sullivan's impromptu assessment had pulled him from that task. "Never mind."

Cal ran his hands along his pants nervously. "That's fine. Long story, right?"

"Are you...?" Ben turned to the friendly attorney he suspected of murder. *Was he trying to bond? At this moment? In this room?* Ben shook his head, gun still keeping watch over his suspect. "Keep your hands up, Cal."

"I didn't do it, remember?"

Ben pointed down the small entryway. "The door is the only way in or out that's been disturbed. No one ran by me in the hall."

"The door was locked."

"You broke it down!" Ben let out a grunt of frustration. Behind him, the clock chimed as it hit 5:30 in the morning. It had been over thirty-two straight hours since he'd felt the embrace of sleep. Every thought of his apartment, however, brought him back to the file waiting for him. The pressure posed by the Grissom File did nothing to aid the murder investigation, especially one that appeared to be connected to the DSA.

"After she was dead."

"How do—" Ben stopped. He could argue all day and get nowhere. Cal wasn't running. He wasn't doing anything more than sitting patiently, waiting for the drained agent to catch up to the situation. Ben had heard the screams. He had trailed them to the upper floor. Then the door fell.

Damn.

Ben's head lowered. "A locked room. So I should expect Sherlock Holmes to make an appearance any second now, right? Come on, Cal Cooper the lawyer. What am I *supposed* to think here?"

Cal's hands rubbed heavily on his knees. He was staring at the silicone-like liquid running down the side of the couch. "I don't want to say."

"Try me."

Cal hesitated, biting his lip. "We don't know each other that well, and the gun thing is really not cementing that 'right side of the law' bond I was hoping for when you walked in so..."

Ben sighed. The gun fell to his side and he tucked it in the back of his pants. "Tell me, Cal."

The young man's eyes softened when he turned to the deceased. His gaze refused to leave her when he spoke and the words chilled Ben as they hung in the air.

"Do you believe in ghosts, Agent Riley?"

CHAPTER SIX

"Keep the change, ya filthy animal." Ben threw a disarming smile at the clerk behind the counter. It was his hope the grin would make the difference if the movie reference landed flat. Even the awkward chuckle he offered next did little to garner favor with the old man that looked exceptionally like Ralph Foody. He remained silent as he passed along the two steaming beverages. Ben pointed to the clock overhead, the display reading 6:16 in bright red. "Too early. I get it."

He left the ten on the counter and departed with the drinks. They felt like furnaces against the bitter cold sweeping through the place. The shop sat directly across from the Edgemont apartment complex and remained one of the few independent shops open at dawn. For six weeks he had done little but look at it in passing. The surveillance placed on him had kept him away. It forced him to look for more open and crowded locations to draw out those tailing him. Since his assessment with Sullivan, Ben hadn't noticed even a single sedan dogging his movements. It was a nice change of pace, and if there was one decent thing that came from the situation Sullivan trapped him in, it was that he finally had an excuse to try out the small-time shop.

A large window ran along the front of the coffee shop. Round tables were positioned throughout the dining area, and the main entry was on the far right. At the corner table farthest from the entrance sat a lone occupant—Ben's guest to the party.

Cal stared outside at the scene unfolding along the street. Three patrol cars were double parked in front of the entrance to the Edgemont. Their lights beamed in a haze of red and blue, cutting through the retreating darkness as the sun slowly rose in the distance. Four uniforms rushed into the building without looking while another worked the radio in his car. The last screamed at a young lady attempting to circumvent the blocked road with a quick trip to the sidewalk.

Ben wanted to be out there with them. Not so much with the bellowing officer, though the woman in the red sedan was quite the looker, but with the ones currently entering the murder scene he had called in. He should have been *leading* the investigation, and in one sense he was, but taking charge brought complications he didn't need at the moment. Leaving the paperwork with the local boys, however, held a certain appeal. It also freed him to pursue the case from an angle not likely noticed or understood by the boys in blue. He sure as hell didn't understand it any better than they did.

But Cal did. *Do you believe in ghosts* was not actually a question in the young man's mind. It was his reality.

Ben cleared his throat, letting the cup in his right hand settle on the edge of the table next to the waiting lawyer. "A tea for the lad talking to spirits. I think you need an upgrade in beverages."

Cal smiled, offering thanks with a raised cup. Ben sat across from him, distracted by the lights outside. "Raspberry ginger tea," Cal announced serenely. "My mother used to make the same blend when I was a kid. Never did like the stuff. The scent, though, always reminds me of those days. Plus, the less caffeine the better."

Ben toasted the memory and sipped his black coffee. The thick beverage caught in his throat and burned the back of his mouth. He winced at the taste.

"You want some?" Cal offered after Ben's display of disgust for his beverage selection.

Ben waved the tea away, forcing another swig of his own strong drink down the hatch before placing it in front of him. "Smoothie bar wasn't open. Too early, I guess. Besides, I think I'll need the extra jolt to keep up with all this."

This. It was easier to think of matters that way. This. That. The other thing. So much easier than coming out and saying the word: ghosts. His childhood nightmares returned to him. He remembered the terrors that had kept him from sleep and the strong words of his father who had tried to make his son a man too soon. Too many expectations back then, too much fear and weakness—always on his end—kept them apart.

"I understand your reticence," Cal said, filling the silence.

"I'm grateful for that," Ben said with a grin. "When I stepped out of my apartment this morning I wondered how much stranger things could get around here. Lo and behold."

"I appreciate the humor, as well as the level of trust you're offering by just sitting with me." He stopped, taking a moment to lick the droplets of tea from the cup's lip. Then he pointed to the flashing lights outside. "You picked this table on purpose, didn't you."

"I did."

Cal leaned back in the chair, exhaling loudly. "You can hand me over if you think that's the right move, Agent Riley. I would understand that too."

"I'm lucky I understand how to work the alarm clock on my cell phone, Cal. Let's just say ghosts might top my bologna radar, but it has quite a bit of company these days."

"Is that your job or something?" the curious lawyer asked, pulling his chair closer. His eyes flitted over the weary agent, never quite landing on the man himself but closer to his shoulders and behind him. "You're some kind of *Weirdness Cop*?"

"Getting that way," he admitted. "But I'm a cop, first and foremost, and you don't have killer written all over you. So, yes, I'm trusting you, but..."

Both turned to the parked patrol cars. Cal nodded. "Got it."

Ben took a long sip from the coffee, letting it heat his entire body. He wished he had taken the time to stop and put on something warmer—an undershirt, even. The quick visit to his apartment had given him only a chance to grab a pair of pants, his sneakers, and his wallet in their rush to vacate the complex before questions could be asked. The coffee would have to do the trick. He took a long breath and leaned close, his voice little more than a whisper. "Talk to me about ghosts, Cal."

Hearing the word, the young lawyer stared off toward the older gentleman near the counter. His eyes intently washed over the subject to the point where Ben was forced to join him. Their collective look shook the man from his work. He reached for a pot of freshly brewed coffee and headed toward the table.

"Cal?" Ben asked curiously. "What is it?"

"Nothing. Don't worry about it."

The old man sharing the same look as the gangster from *Home Alone* stopped short. Ben smiled at him, welcoming him to their table. The man was missing the second button on his shirt, and his glasses hung from a line of thin plastic around his neck.

"Top you off there?" the old man inquired. Ben held out his cup. He concealed his distaste for the drink beneath the smile. The beverage wasn't needed. A caffeine headache settled in, but he maintained his gratitude for courtesy's sake.

"You lost a button."

Both men peered at Cal; both were interested in his observation, but for different reasons. The old man shrugged. "Must have popped off."

Cal nodded, his eyes never wavering. They were leveled on the clerk, yet at the same time they weren't. Almost as if the young lawyer from Albany was looking just right of the man.

"You should check in the vanity," Cal continued. "A little red box on the top shelf."

The old man's hand shook, the pot of coffee threatening to fall. "I'm sorry?"

"What was her name?" Cal pointed to the ring on the man's finger. "Your wife?"

"She—"

"Lorraine, right?"

The shocked proprietor leaned hard against the table. "How could you possibly know that?"

Cal moved to speak, but he was cut off by Ben's sudden laughter rising in the air. The anxious agent patted the old man's arm lightly in jest. "It's a magic trick, sir. That's all."

"Ah." He paused for a moment before stepping back from the table. "You had me there."

The clerk moved for the counter, a short shuffle with each step that threatened to topple him over. He turned back as Cal called to him, saying, "Sir. Wait. I'd be a heel if I didn't mention this."

Ben cleared his throat, a glare sending his message across the table. Cal sighed under his breath. With a slight nod he lifted his beverage high and smiled. "This tea is delicious. Thank you."

Ben waited until the gentleman retreated behind the counter before leaning close to the table. "Well that was unnecessary."

Cal ran a hand through his hair. "I know."

"You scared the crap out of him."

"It's a gift."

Frustration hid behind Cal's eyes. They held the agony that came from what he could see and what he did with the information offered. "So how does this work? She's here, right? Lorraine?"

"That's not a name you hear much anymore."

"Cal."

He took a long sip, his eyes trailing off. The old man across the room rubbed at the missing button. His memories distracted him from their conversation. "She's here. He lives above this place, and she did as well. Twenty years. Worked here every day. She died in her sleep six months ago. Not exactly the happiest person, much to her regret."

"What was it you were going to say to him?"

Somber stares continued; lost youth filled his sky-blue orbs. "She's worried about him. He's forgetting things, and she wants him to retire. Go somewhere. Do something else while he can. Her language is… a little more colorful."

Ben slipped back in his chair. He looked to the owner of the shop, and then to his companion. "This is what you do? See them? Talk to them?"

Cal's head lowered. "I was in an accident when I was eighteen. Dumb kid move. Driving like a maniac. I was angry, had something to prove. Whatever excuse you want.

"There was this curve along the woods south of my parent's house. Must have driven that way a hundred times before that night, but when it came up it was like it had never been there before. I broke through the guard rail doing eighty. The car dropped twenty feet into a gulch. I should have died. Instead, this happened." Cal pulled back his mussed-up hair. A scar ran near his scalp. "I woke up in the hospital to the sound of voices. Only there wasn't anyone else in the room with me. Somehow the accident opened a door for me to the other side."

Ghosts. Even entertaining the concept as a reality frightened Ben, but as he stacked it against a man with the power to create flames and a signal capable of turning people into trees, it was hard to draw a line in the sand dividing reality and fantasy.

"You think a ghost killed Winslow?"

Cal drained his cup, then placed it on the table. "Are you asking for my help, Agent Riley?"

Ben tapped his foot quickly, his head throbbing. Both recalled the gun pointed at Cal less than an hour earlier. He needed answers, and the man across from him appeared to be the only open avenue for getting them. At least for the moment. "You do what I say when I say it, and if I think any of this has gone off the rails... Wow. That was a terrible choice of words. Sorry."

"No worries," Cal replied without care.

"If I feel we've crossed the line of reason, so much as one can when dealing with..." Ben glanced around the room, suddenly unsure how far his voice carried. "Do we really just call them ghosts?"

"Among other names. Yes."

"Do they call themselves ghosts?"

"Never," Cal answered. "And you should never say it to their face."

Ben scratched his head. "Duly noted."

"You're easily sidetracked, Agent Riley. Is it the caffeine?"

"Yeah," Ben said, rubbing his head. "Wired to the brim here."

Cal smiled. "I want to help, Agent."

"Better make it Ben. I'm glad you're on board, but do you truly believe that's what happened to Winslow?"

"Yes, but you don't, so..." Cal stood, took half a step toward the door, then stopped to throw Ben a wave. "Let's ask her."

CHAPTER SEVEN

Morgan checked her watch. Each second ticked by like the beat of a drum behind her eyes. She stood at the entrance to her apartment, a hand on the knob.

"This is ridiculous."

Zac had left almost an hour ago. Afterward, she collected her clothes from their wild night and set about preparing for her day, just as she should have done from the start. Without distraction. *But, oh what a distraction…*

Now, though, she hesitated at the door. If she arrived at the office too closely to Zac would people notice? A ludicrous assumption, yet his very name brought out her pearly whites in a wide grin.

It was silly, to say the least: the notion that anyone noticed or cared about their comings and goings or who arrived with whom. It locked in her head and refused to abate. Much like the entire night.

Never in a million years would she have believed such a thing possible. Never would she have imagined sharing her bed with anyone from work, let alone the geeky Head of Operational Support and Research.

Yet it had happened.

Not only that, but she couldn't stop thinking about their time together—and about the possibility of it happening again. The thought alone maintained the smile already across her lips, lips that still felt the soft touch of the man she had invited to her home.

What was I thinking? She didn't know. Zac had helped reconnect her with her family in Baltimore. Years had been spent in exile, and now connections were rekindled and dinners were scheduled. He had stayed by her side and listened to her fall from grace, the loss of her medical license and so much more. He had supported her through it all. No one had ever done that for her before.

She had been taught at a young age to stand on her own, to rely on no one, to trust less. Throughout their time together she had pushed him away, kept her distance from him—even recently, while trying to save his life in Chicago. He had persisted. When he looked at her it was with compassion. She could tell from the softness of his fingers on her shoulder and the soulful gaze in his eyes.

Their night together felt right to her; it had been a perfect moment.

Morgan wasn't sure what he was thinking, though, and it troubled her. While she carried no attachments to consider after their rendezvous, Zac was married. He had a kid; he had a life. There was happiness every time he mentioned his family. Knowing that, she had still made the invitation to him. And he had accepted.

That meant something, didn't it?

Morgan let it lie, checking her watch again. Another four minutes had passed while she was lost in the memory of the last few hours. Plenty of time to throw off any suspicion—not that any existed. She turned the handle on the door, releasing the oak from the frame.

"Agent Dunleavy."

Morgan jumped back at the sight of Susan Metcalf, Director of the DSA, standing in the hallway. Her hand was raised with the intention to knock, and a file was tucked under her left arm.

"Cripes," Morgan cursed, attempting to wipe the drips of coffee streaming down her fingers. "You scared a year off my life."

"Not my intention."

"I would hope not," Morgan said. "What are you—?"

Metcalf shifted past the surprised agent and entered the apartment. "May I come in?"

"I... I was about to head into the office."

Metcalf waited at the kitchen counter. She slipped her jacket off and placed it on one of the twin stools positioned between the kitchen and living room. "Not necessary now."

The curious director paced the apartment slowly. Morgan blinked hard at the circumstances, then rested her coffee atop the counter. As Metcalf neared the bedroom, Morgan leapt in front of her. The sheets had been ripped from the bed, the curtains still closed, and the scent of her activities would be too noticeable. She quickly slammed the door shut.

"Laundry day."

Metcalf paused, curiosity in her eyes. Then she shifted back to the counter with a shrug. "You should hire a service."

"Why are we talking here instead of your office?" Morgan circled the counter to face Metcalf.

"Right to it, then." The director removed the file from under her arm and held it out to the curious agent. "I need your help with something."

"Okay," Morgan said, drawing out the word. She took the file in hand without opening it. "So same question, this time about the briefing room."

"I can't make it official," Metcalf answered, her voice soft. "I'd handle this myself, but my hands are currently tied."

There was something in Metcalf's eyes that worried Morgan—something never seen in the strong woman who had served as her superior since she started at the DSA. Metcalf was a brick wall, holding everything together. Morgan had always taken that to be the coldness she displayed for the world. The detachment required to make the tough calls no one else could.

The look had angered Morgan for a time after Grissom's death. Morgan had lost a good friend, a man who had pulled her out of the gutter and given her hope where there had been none. Anger and resentment were natural during that time. Questions remained over Grissom's actions that had led to his untimely demise. She still didn't know whether or not the secret objective to retrieve dangerous samples came directly from Metcalf without the rest of the team's knowledge.

Over the weeks it had slowly faded—not the loss, not the second guessing over what happened, but the blame placed at Metcalf's feet. In a world of difficult choices she faced the absolute toughest without complaint, without hesitation. Now when Morgan looked at her superior, she saw the mortar chipping away. Wrinkles ran from once-sharp, now-tired eyes. Morgan understood the politics of their work. Hands tied for the director meant there was maneuvering going on at a level well above Morgan's pay grade. It was taking a toll on the stalwart head of the DSA.

"Riley joining me?"

"He's out of reach." The answer came too quick. Metcalf's gaze fell away, a play at returning to her scan of the apartment. Both, however, recognized her swift response to be a lie. It was one Metcalf refused to acknowledge, loudly clearing her throat before pushing ahead. "I believe you're better suited for it. Alone."

Morgan raised her left brow. "Sounds ominous enough."

"It is," Metcalf said. "Something happened in Des Moines."

Morgan put the file between them and opened it. An array of photos greeted her, images of the dead interspersed throughout. Two bodies, both male, murdered without prejudice. She continued to flip through the packet of reports. She stopped at the image of the suspected murderer fleeing the scene of the crime.

Lincoln.

Panicked eyes flew to her superior. "When did this —?"

"Yesterday. I would have informed you immediately, however —"

"I needed the day." Morgan waved her off. "We're sure this is Lincoln?"

"Definitely," Metcalf admitted. "The motive behind it, though, is at the top of my list of questions."

"Questions you want me to ask him," Morgan said.

"Yes."

Morgan held tight to the image of Lincoln taken from surveillance. He had been at the Savery Hotel in Des Moines. She knew what the site meant to him. He'd shared the story with her during a stakeout almost a year earlier. Crazed eyes marked the photo; his posture was defensive. He was decked out in black fatigues, and the vest and armaments gave him a war-like visage.

"What was he doing there?" she asked as she dropped the photo on top of the report. Morgan suddenly remembered the missed calls from days earlier. Lincoln had phoned her out of the blue. No message, but the calls alone were suspicious. She had been unable to answer due to their case in Chicago. Had they been a warning to her? A cry for help? "Metcalf? He wouldn't just take off and start killing people."

Metcalf remained stoic. "He was on assignment."

Morgan waited impatiently for a long moment for more information. None was forthcoming. Her hand slapped the file shut. "I'm not playing this game. You want me to find Lincoln, I want to know what the hell is going on. What assignment?"

Metcalf let out a long breath, and her hands fell to her hips. "He was tracking someone on my authority."

"Who?"

"The Witness."

"The nutjob from Bellbrook?" Morgan questioned. Surprise and anger welled in her, and she fought to contain both. *The man who killed Ruth Heller? The man who slaughtered a town with the press of a button?* "You sent him after that psychopath without any backup?"

"I did."

"You regretting that decision now?"

Metcalf grimaced. "I am."

"Damn right you are," Morgan snapped, snatching the file for a closer look. "Who did he kill and please let that creep with the glasses top the list."

"Unfortunately, no." Metcalf shook her head in disappointment. "The dead weren't exactly victims in this, no matter the appearance in the report. They were hunting our quarry as well. Their names are listed in the file, but they won't lead you to Lincoln."

Nothing would unless Lincoln wanted to be found. Metcalf, however, was right about the deceased in Des Moines. Their names were about all that had been released to the public. Everything else had been flagged and redacted. She recognized the language used throughout. Military code. They were soldiers.

Morgan closed the thin folder, her hand resting firmly atop. "I'll find him."

"I know you will," Metcalf replied. Her stare softened with the timbre of her voice. She appeared broken compared to the proud woman Morgan once held in high esteem.

"The department is in the dark on this?"

Metcalf nodded. "With good reason. They won't give Lincoln a second to explain, or allow him to find a way back from this. We can give that to him—if he gives us the Witness."

"Agreed."

"I can't offer any support on this. It has to be you. On your own."

Morgan slipped her coat on and grabbed her keys. The coffee in one hand and the file in the other, she started for the door. "He'll talk to me, Susan. We can fix this."

"He doesn't get a choice in the matter, Morgan. I need him to understand that. There's only one way out of this mess for him."

They both knew Lincoln better than that. How he thought. How he operated. And what he might do if he was trapped in a corner.

"If he refuses?"

Metcalf's eyes thinned. "See that he doesn't. Any way you have to."

CHAPTER EIGHT

Dawn broke over the Edgemont. The clouds overhead changed from deep pink to orange. Ben made his way across the street, the clanging of the bell inside the coffee shop fading behind him. Cal followed, though his steps were short and hesitant compared to the rapid pace set by the DSA agent. Ben wanted to get back to the scene as quickly as possible. His eyes stayed locked on the vehicles blocking the road. A fourth joined the mix, this one a black sedan with precinct plates. Ben sipped his coffee while he walked, always a mistake, and the steaming liquid dribbled down his chin.

"I'm not an expert on the subject," Cal said. Ben reached for the front door to the apartment building, then held it open for his new colleague. Cal stopped near the sidewalk, staring up at the populated structure. "I've spent my entire adult life avoiding it."

"I can imagine." Ben understood all right. No scenario existed in his mind to explain some of the things witnessed during his tenure at the DSA. Cal's *gift*, however, was on another level altogether. "But there are experts on ghosts?"

"A few," the lawyer from Albany answered. "Well, quite a few, but only a couple you can actually talk to without calling an orderly to tighten the straitjacket."

"Great retirement plan."

"It's something I think about more than I'd like."

Ben viewed Cal's reticence with curiosity. Fatigue filled his eyes, deeper than any Ben held that morning. The weariness went back years for Cal, to the accident that had robbed him of the sense of normalcy most people clung to tighter than their wallets on the subway.

"Well, I really hope you're wrong," Ben said. "That our killer is a run-of-the-mill corporeal nutjob."

Cal shook his head. He approached slowly, letting Ben enter the building first while taking hold of the glass door. "It's not. Did you see the goop by the windows running down the sill? More by the couch—thanks for making me sit there, by the way. Not to mention the cold spots near the body? Definitely not run of the mill."

Ben started for the stairs at the end of the elongated lobby. It remained empty due to the hour, though the sound of movement bled through the thin walls as the residents started their days. "Walk me through what you can."

At the base of the stairs, Ben stopped. He turned back to see Cal still at the entrance. The young man took long breaths, his eyes flitting through the wide space; he appeared overwhelmed by the sight of emptiness.

"Cal?"

"Sorry." Cal nodded, letting the door slide from his grip. His foot fell with finality as he took a large first step inside. "Not a fan of apartment buildings as a rule. Lot of people in a small space."

"On both sides of the fence?"

Cal shuffled toward the stairs. Every few steps, he pivoted, shifting right or left and tucking his arms in front of him to avoid a collision though no one was present in the space. Ben squinted, hoping for some sign, some assurance that the young man accompanying him was on the level. He appreciated Cal's confidence in the situation, yet the fears of Ben's childhood returned alongside the thought of what remained unseen and hidden from view.

Ben tapped along the base of the railing until Cal finished his dance through the lobby. The attorney sighed, digging his hands deeper into his pockets.

"I had a house built to avoid this. Nothing extravagant. A small ranch on a heavily researched plot of land. It was the only way I could get some sleep."

"It didn't stop you before."

"True. Damsel in distress syndrome?" Ben's eyebrow creased, causing his companion to shake his head. "No, I know. I guess I wasn't thinking about it at the time."

Ben stopped at the second floor landing, letting a tired gentleman with a crooked tie and coffee-stained shirt stumble past them. Cal moved for the next floor, but Ben's hand caught him on his shoulder and held him back.

"Wait a minute," Ben said. "What *were* you doing here?" It was the first question he should have asked upon finding Cal in the apartment of the deceased Abigail Winslow. Or, at the very least, the first question that should have been asked after learning the young lawyer hailed from New York and not the eighth floor of the Edgemont. Cal's eyes fell, his gaze sullen and distant. "You knew her."

"I was watching her," Cal admitted, wincing at the immediate look Ben threw to him. "Hey. Nothing creepy like that. She was one of the FBI agents that worked on a case that's personal to me."

Personal had a few connotations to it, but one jumped out for Ben immediately. "Something to do with your family?"

Cal nodded and kept his head low.

"What happened?"

"They died." Cal held tight to the railing as they climbed. "Every last one of them, in fact. Going on a year now."

Ben almost fell down the flight of stairs. How had he not made the connection? "Hold it. Cal Cooper? The Cooper Massacre in Albany? *That* Cooper?"

"That Cooper."

A holiday party turned into a slaughterhouse. Every member of the affluent Cooper line had died. Men, women, and children. No discernible reason. No trace of poison in their systems, though it was some time before their bodies were discovered. Only one person from the family had survived and only because he wasn't present—making him the prime suspect for months afterward. Cal's name had flashed on television screens across the country after the massacre, his name synonymous with either death or luck, depending on your view of the event.

No evidence existed to convict or even charge. Questions plagued the affair, and still did. Questions from both police and the shattered young man at Ben's side.

"They never found out who did it."

Cal kept his eyes straight ahead. Their travels carried them swiftly to the eighth-floor landing and the corridor beyond. "Or how they did it. Or why they did it."

"I'm sorry," Ben whispered, regretful at mentioning it. "It takes a lot to keep going, I would imagine."

"I get by," Cal said, though the words were distant.

"Yeah?" Ben stopped at the bend in the hall. Three apartments down on the left was their destination. The caved-in door had been replaced by a makeshift police barricade. Cal's breathing slowed. Ben waited patiently for more, the picture of his colleague suddenly coming into view for the first time.

"Anyway," Cal started, refusing to catch Ben's glare. "Agent Winslow's name popped up on some of the reports I was able to procure with some legal maneuvering. For some reason she never filed her own though. I was curious about that."

"And you happened to be here today of all days?"

"I am lucky that way," Cal said. He rubbed the back of his neck. "I was in town for a consult. A favor for a friend of the family. Winslow walked by me at the airport and I recognized her from some crime scene photos."

"Good memory."

Cal shook his head. "It's been my nightstand reading, if you know what I mean."

He did. Ben knew very well what it meant to be so wrapped up in an obsession, a single question with a myriad of answers—none completely fitting and no perfect solution presenting itself. A single case that overshadowed all others. In Buffalo it was the house on Wex, the place his career and his life had both ended. Part of him would always be in that house until the mystery was solved. His current concern, however, rested on the desk in his apartment. Cal carried his mystery everywhere he went and had been for a year.

"Right." Ben clapped his hands, forcing a grin. "So these rules?"

Cal chuckled at the term. "Yes. The *rules*. A close friend served as an advocate for years before retiring. He learned quite a bit about the other side."

"Advocate?"

"For the dead. You see, spirits are subject to the same societal rules that existed before death. Violent crimes are punished, although there can be hoops to jump through to make it happen on the back end. Paperwork is a bitch, even in the afterlife."

Ben stood mystified. "You make it sound normal. Like walking down the street."

"It is," Cal replied. He stopped every few seconds, peering along the hallway. His gaze settled on a specific spot with each pass before he returned to the man at his side. "The dead infest this world. Most are afraid to keep going to whatever comes next. Some have a reason to stay behind. Loved ones. Revenge. The usual grab bag. Mostly, though, there is no unfinished business tying them here. They are either too scared or too pissed off over their lives to let go."

"And Winslow?"

"With violent deaths, in particular, the victims are rooted to the scene of their deaths. It's the trauma of the moment. They are stuck at a specific place, most screaming for justice. Where other spirits might return to their childhood home or other perfect moment from their pasts, victims of violent crimes are locked to their deaths like a beacon."

"So we go talk to her? Just like that?"

Cal peered into the emptiness of the corridor. His words were heavy with sadness. "Just like that."

Ben rubbed his chin, trying to process it all. Then he reached into his pocket and removed the thin badge. "You going to be okay with this?"

Cal nodded. "Yeah. I'm good."

Ben hitched his thumb toward the open door and the waiting officers within. "Let's dial her up, then, shall we?"

CHAPTER NINE

Ben casually approached the open door to the apartment. Several officers surveyed the scene within the domicile. Others canvassed the hall for more information, while another stood solemnly at the edge of the room. The last carried a notepad and pen, his head tilted to the right to see the room clearly over his burgeoning gut. Ben tapped on the frame that had housed the fallen door, causing grumbles to escape the man's lips. He waddled to the door while tucking his pad in his breast pocket. Ben displayed his badge with a smile, his companion watching from the end of the corridor.

"I need the room," Ben said before the man could say a word. He tried to save time, to beat out the inevitable argument. As he read the man's reaction, Ben regretted the tactic immediately.

"This is an active crime scene, mister…" The man's voice was hoarse; a bullfrog seemed to be permanently trapped in his well-hidden neck.

"Agent," Ben corrected, the badge pushed closer to the officer's face. "I'm with the DSA."

"You're with who? How did you even hear about this already?"

"Doesn't matter." Ben tucked his identification away. "Above your pay grade. Look. I'm not kicking you out, Officer—"

"Detective," the man said. His badge read the name Rutnall in bold letters.

"Detective. Of course." Ben's eyes never left Rutnall, the message clear between them: the veiled threat of demotion. Rutnall's cheeks reddened at the mystery agent in the doorway.

He cleared his throat. "It sounds like you're kicking us out."

"I need five minutes."

The anger continued to rise in Rutnall's cheeks. "I have jurisdiction on this."

"You really don't," Ben replied. "She was one of ours."

The detective fell silent. He glanced at the scene and the three men searching the apartment. Forensics was on its way and would arrive soon. Photos would be taken, and the press would follow. Both understood the way it would play on camera with a victim having no obvious cause of death.

What Rutnall also realized—what Ben counted on in mentioning Winslow's affiliation—was how jurisdiction shifted with a single call. It was not a ploy or a card to play. There was no gaming Rutnall with the information. When one of their own fell in the line it was a sign of respect in the profession to allow access. It was an opportunity to stand side by side in the pursuit of justice for those lost.

Rutnall understood, only able to utter a solitary, "Oh."

"Yeah," Ben replied, keeping his voice low. "Listen, Detective. You can have it. Honest. I just need five minutes to see if I get the joy of telling the bosses we have a security threat."

Rutnall's eyes widened. "Security threat?"

Ben leaned close to the man. "You know what the DSA handles, Rutnall?"

The detective fell back a step; he was no longer flush with anger, but filled with concern. "No. Why?"

Ben patted his shoulder with a smirk. "You don't *want* to know."

Rutnall paused, taking Ben's measure. Time was an issue. This was about more than a murder in the portly detective's mind. Ben inserted the security issue as another watchword for the man, but other factors played a part, the least of which was who claimed jurisdiction over the scene. It could go two ways. For Rutnall it was either a feather in his cap at the capture of a clever killer or—if Ben was denied access—a battle with an unknown agency working at a higher clearance than he wanted to consider.

In regard to all aspects, weighed and accounted for, the decision became simple. Rutnall drew aside, giving Ben as much room as possible in the slight hall of the apartment.

"Thanks." Ben stepped inside, then paused, throwing a wave

to his colleague. "We'll be quick."

"We?" Rutnall asked, his voice cracking.

Cal grinned. Ben patted Rutnall's shoulder once more. "A consultant. Nothing to worry about."

"If you say so," Rutnall said with a nod. He caught sight of the other officers on site and waved them toward the door.

Ben threw a grateful nod to each as they passed, curious looks bearing down on him in growing degrees. Finally, only Rutnall remained. He stood fixed in the hall, unable or unwilling to move in either direction.

"Five minutes, Detective. Thanks."

For a moment Ben believed another argument tipped the tongue of the stout officer of the law. Instead, only grumbling escaped Rutnall's lips, the fight growing more distant with each labored breath.

"A real badge would help," the young attorney jested as he led them toward the waiting body.

"Don't I know it." He peered at the officers circling the door, questions murmured to Rutnall under their breaths. "They'll be back in three. How does this work?"

"It's not a ritual, Ben."

"Good," Ben said, patting his pockets. "Fresh out of candles."

"Just give me a—" He was cut off by the sound of a phone ringing. The shrill tone echoed from Ben's breast pocket throughout the sparsely decorated apartment. Both men jumped at the noise. Cal threw a hard look to the disruptive agent. "Really?"

Ben shrugged, pulling the phone loose from his pocket. He moved for the spare bedroom to give Cal the room. The phone continued to blare, but the clock on the display kept his attention. He made Cal aware of their time restraint with two raised fingers, then closed the door.

Metcalf's personal cell showed on the display below the time and date. The number was accompanied by an image of Anne Ramsey from *Throw Momma from the Train*. The bright image of the scowling figure brought a smile to Ben's lips.

"She's not a woman… she's the Terminator."

When the ringing ended, he let out a relieved breath. The device began to ring once again within seconds, voicemail apparently not an option for the belligerent Director of the DSA. Ben held the phone out for a long moment. They needed to have a chat. The way things had been left after his meeting with Sullivan and Stallworth made that clear. He knew what had happened to Grissom, as well as Metcalf's role in the affair. There was more to the story, but he didn't need the lie of it. The story she'd refined since seeing him at Fort Meade.

He also couldn't handle the truth either. A man had fallen in the line of duty, left to die by an uncaring supervisor. Or so the story went, according to the evidence. Now Ben held the man's position and there was no way he would go out the same way. Trusting the DSA to handle Winslow's death might have been the right play, but it wasn't how Ben viewed matters. Especially not after bringing Cal into the mix. Too many questions remained about the young man. Ben decided to handle the case without the agency's support for now.

He ignored the call and turned off the phone. Slipping it into his pocket, he stepped deeper into the spare bedroom belonging to the deceased. The window remained open. Ben grabbed a pair of gloves left by the officers and lowered the sash into the frame, ending the breeze whipping through the room.

The view held him in place. His apartment sat directly across the way. A clear shot of his bedroom and the spare room where the Grissom File lay open on his desk. All visible from her window. Unnerving, but not so much as the tripod positioned in front of the sill. Ben circled the bed and a glint of metal caught his attention. He reached into the shadows and retrieved a closed case. After he placed it on the bed to open the clasp, photo equipment spilled out along the mattress. Telephoto lenses, a multitude of filters, and data drives—all necessary equipment for surveilling his apartment.

Why?

The question rang in his mind, buried beneath the soft rapping at the door. Cal peered in, his head tilting toward the living area.

"Did I miss the show?" Ben asked, joining his colleague.

"There was none," Cal admitted.

"What do you mean?"

"She's not here."

"You said—" Ben said. He cut himself off at the sight of Rutnall glancing from the shattered entryway.

"I know," Cal muttered. The two shifted to the far side of the living room. The window ledge remained slick with the silicone-like goop previously seen, a trail flowing beneath to the green carpet. "I know what I said. Her murder should have linked her spirit to this scene. She *should* be here, screaming at me about who killed her."

"But she's not," Ben said. "That means what, exactly?"

Cal's hand moved for his lips. "No. Oh, no."

"That sounds less than promising."

The young lawyer scratched his chin. His loafers paced the room, his eyes locked on the dead woman. "Her spirit isn't here."

"We know that, Cal."

"No. I mean it isn't here so it isn't *anywhere*. She wasn't simply murdered physically, but spiritually as well."

"How does that…?" Ben started to ask before realizing how underwater he had become with this case. He didn't understand the questions that needed asking. He only knew there was a killer on the loose. "What the hell can do that?"

Cal stopped in the center of the room. "That's where the news gets worse."

Ben read the look of worry in his colleague's eyes. "You know what this is. That's something, isn't it?"

"The worst kind of something." Cal crouched next to the dead woman. His fingers hovered over her thin locks of black hair, spread wide from where she fell.

"What is it, Cal?"

"Something we can't stop." The lawyer turned to face Ben, eyes heavy with fear. The feeling was shared by the overwhelmed DSA agent. "It's a specter."

CHAPTER TEN

Zac skirted through the closing doors of the warehouse, one hand attempting to tuck in his shirt and the other clutched tight to his laptop bag. His tardiness sent pangs of guilt up his spine, and his cheeks darkened with each tick of the clock. The front guard joked about his imitation of a raspberry.

Zac made no reply. The clock may have played a role in his distraction, but it was not the true reason.

Had it really happened? Was it only a figment of his incredibly vivid imagination? Her scent lingered around him; it infected his clothes, which were wrinkled and wishing for a laundry cycle. It was real—the perfect night.

But was it something he would have pursued if not invited by the ebony-skinned goddess who now filled his every waking thought? Never. He desired her but had no drive—no impulse to make the first move. Yet now all he wanted was to return to her arms. To walk right back out of work, tardiness be damned, and surround himself with her touch, her heat, her everything.

What is wrong with me? I have a wife!

It was a complication lost to the events of their lovemaking. Claire and Alex—his family. The one thing he swore above all others when he committed to his college sweetheart: a promise to be faithful. Six years he'd managed without a stray glance, without pause or question. Honest and true in every way. Then with one temptation, everything was ruined.

His smile, the one carried from Morgan's apartment more than an hour earlier, finally faded. Once he was past the security gate and down the entry hall to the analyst hub, Zac paused. His back settled along the wall, and the consequences of his fling bore down on him harder than if the building had collapsed at that exact second. From perfection to complicated. From weightless to guilt-ridden in every respect. The Zac Modine model of problem solving.

"I have to tell her," he muttered under his breath. Stray glances broke his way from a pair of researchers refilling their coffee at the sputtering machine across the corridor. False grins passed between both parties, and Zac pushed off the wall for his waiting office.

'Office' was a stretch. Operations rested in the basement of the complex. Monitors ran along the south wall, stations and consoles allowing the team to track the field team's bio-metrics as well as their mission parameters. Sometimes there were more than twenty individuals in the room: tracking, observing, and assisting members in the field. Without a mission in play, typically the number fell to one or two.

Usually only one.

Zac had requested a personal space to work. It was granted so an office was created in the room. In actuality the privacy granted by the cubicle wall around his metal desk did little to keep people out of his hair. More often than not it was a beacon to those in his employ as well as his superiors to his whereabouts at all times.

Alison Adler completed a routine check of the systems in place, tablet before her chest. She caught sight of Zac's lingering shadow at the door and joined him, a curious look on her face.

"You wore that yesterday."

"I'm aware," Zac grumbled. He started for his desk, though he was cut off by his direct subordinate.

"Yet you did it anyway?" she pressed. Adler was a new addition to his team in Operations. She had been recruited by Metcalf to serve as Zac's immediate backup—a position he believed to be unnecessary and dubious. Her very presence made him doubt the sanctity of the protocols he'd spent years building. She made him doubt *everything* about the DSA, something he never imagined possible.

Much like his perfect night, already subsumed by the dawn of the new day.

"Never made it home," Zac replied with clenched teeth. "Long night."

"Uh-huh."

Zac huffed. "I was working, Adler."

The young woman shrugged. "I said, uh-huh, as sarcastically as I could manage."

There was no telling her otherwise. The story was written in his wrinkled shirt, still untucked on one side. It screamed at Adler in bold letters in his messy hair, in his inability to make eye contact to address a simple question. It didn't matter what excuse he had ready to run from his lips.

Zac decided changing the subject played better than continuing to flub his lies. "Any updates?"

"All good in the hood."

Zac rolled his eyes. "Please don't say that again."

"Yeah," Adler replied with a nod. "It didn't land."

"Not at all."

Zac backed into his cubicle, letting his laptop bag settle on the floor next to him. "I'll check out the queue and see how we're running."

Adler's eyes flared. She pointed at his waiting desk. "Oh, there's—"

"Good morning, Mr. Modine," a shadow greeted Zac at his terminal. Greg Sullivan sat back in Zac's chair with an air of satisfaction and a smile. Zac reeled, surprised at the elder gentleman's ability to sneak around the warehouse with such ease. His glare shifted to Adler and thinned.

The young woman played with her tablet innocently. "There might be someone here to see you. And yes, I should have led with that."

"Thanks, Adler."

"Happy to help," she announced, then quickly moved for the door. She threw a wave on her way. "I'll be overseeing the hub if you need me."

The silence hung over the room in Adler's absence. Zac gathered his laptop bag from the edge of the cubicle wall, strangling the strap for all it was worth. The silence was a plus, but what he truly desired was a second to catch his breath from his night. A shower and the time to change into his emergency clothes kept hanging behind his desk would have been appreciated as well. Frankly, he didn't need the company at the moment.

Zac bit his lip then forced a smile when he faced the deputy director again. "We have to stop meeting like this, sir."

Sullivan smirked, resting comfortably in the man's chair. "That would be a pleasant change of pace."

"What can I—?"

"Your wife called," Sullivan interrupted.

"My wife?" Zac asked, his voice choking to get the words out.

"Claire, I believe?"

"Claire," Zac repeated. Heat flooded every inch of his skin. He sat the laptop against the desk, then reached for the wall for extra support. "My wife, Claire. She… she called?"

"She did," Sullivan said. He seemed to perk up at the tech's stuttering. A devilish grin grew as he leaned along the edge of the desk with his hands clasped in front of him. "Lovely woman. She was just checking in, making sure everything was all right. Something about an abrupt end to your last chat. I informed her you were indisposed at the time."

"Indisposed? I—"

"I assume your hands were full somewhere in this massive tomb of a building," Sullivan continued. His eyes swelled, the deep black in the center peered straight through the sweating subordinate. Zac fought for breath, swiping at his brow. "Or perhaps you were working off-site?"

Does he know? Zac wondered, almost asking out loud as if that was the right move. What could he say? *Claire…*

"Right," Zac said. He left the safety of the cubicle wall, puffing out his chest and clearing his throat. "Yes, thank you. I'll have to call her."

"Of course." Sullivan stood from the desk, slow steps bringing him before Zac. The overweight tech was thankful for the dim lights masking the massive amount of perspiration running through his uncombed hair. Sullivan stopped beside him. "You're an asset to this team, Zac. I've said as much before. I hope you know you have my utmost confidence in getting the job done."

"I… Thank you, sir."

"Others don't show you enough appreciation for the work you provide," Sullivan said. "Director Metcalf, for one."

Zac had mentioned his issues with the director previously out of anger. It was a slip of the tongue he wished he could take back—to tuck away and swallow rather than let anyone see that side of him again. He had been bitter about secrets kept from him. Disappointed in the actions of his superior, whom he admired for so long. The pedestal had crumbled over the last few months.

"About that, sir," Zac started. "I never should have—"

"You were being honest, Zac. No shame in that." Sullivan's eyes went cold, the smug grin gone in an instant. "Now I would like to do the same with you. If you'll allow me, that is?"

"Sir?"

Sullivan pointed to the waiting computer screen. He led the tech to the chair. Zac took the invitation, sliding in along the desk. Sullivan shook the mouse and the monitor came to life.

"Susan has crossed a line," Sullivan said as he cycled through directories. Zac attempted to keep the man in view while reading the files flipping by rapidly. "Bellbrook and Chicago were missteps. No one doubts that, least of all yourself. This Lincoln situation—and thank you for bringing me up to speed on it—has confirmed my worst fears about her."

He had disobeyed orders, broken protocol, to send Sullivan the initial reports coming out of Des Moines. It was Metcalf's job to do so, not his, but his lack of trust in her and the fear of her secrets had forced him to take action.

"What are you trying to say, sir?"

Sullivan stopped, then pushed away from the desk. The light of the monitor washed over the proud deputy director. "Lincoln murdered two men in cold blood—two men who served our country proudly in the military. He also allowed a terrorist to escape custody. What is being done about it?"

"I don't know. Director Metcalf—"

"Sent him there in the first place," Sullivan said, anger in his voice. "Do you doubt that?"

"No," Zac admitted. It pained him to say it, but the evidence was clear. It was an unsanctioned operation—something out of the question at one time. There had been no oversight, no support of any kind. That wasn't what he'd signed on for when he joined the department.

"She needs to be replaced," Sullivan said. "For the sake of the DSA. For the protection of every man and woman in this building. For their families. For Claire. Don't you agree?"

Zac's gaze fell to the floor. They were talking about treason of the highest order, a mutiny within the ranks of the department. He had dedicated the last five years of his life to the DSA. Every day had been a privilege. Then Grissom fell. It was followed quickly by the event in Bellbrook and Ruth Heller's death. Secrets and lies slowly took over every aspect of the agency.

"Yes," he answered, his voice soft yet clear in the emptiness of the room.

"Zac, she's working against us even now. Lincoln needs to be taken into custody to face his crimes. What is Susan doing about it?"

"Like I said, I don't—"

"Allow me," the deputy director interjected. He clicked the mouse and a file opened on the screen. It was a surveillance recording, the date and time from only an hour earlier. Zac panicked when he saw the location.

Morgan Dunleavy's apartment.

"You're monitoring—"

"Listen," Sullivan said, finger to his lips.

"The department is in the dark on this?" Morgan's voice chirped through the speaker. She leaned along the kitchen counter where only hours earlier the two of them had shared more than one intimate kiss. Metcalf had her back to the camera, but it was clearly the director in all her glory.

"With good reason. They won't give Lincoln a second to explain, or allow him to find a way back from this. We can give that to him — if he gives us the Witness."

"Agreed."

Metcalf's words were lost under Morgan's movements for her coat; the sensitivity of the bug in the apartment had been set too high. The error probably came from either a lack of training or a lack of time in setting the device. Unfortunately, Morgan's reply came back clear, creating a deep pit in Zac's stomach.

"He'll talk to me, Susan. We can fix this."

Sullivan ended the playback. "I know it might be tough to hear, especially today, but Agent Dunleavy's loyalties should be thoroughly questioned in this matter. Who knows how many others are involved in this as well."

"What?" the overwhelmed tech choked. "What are you saying?"

"You heard them, Zac," Sullivan said. "They are working against the mandate of this agency. The evidence is mounting against Susan and her loyalists. I'm here because I need to know where you stand."

"I..." Zac returned to the monitor. Morgan captured the screen, her presence all encompassing. So beautiful in her strength, such power in her every word. Every word going against his beliefs in the DSA.

Their night had been perfect, everything he'd ever dreamed of, but that was all it turned out to be in the end. A dream. This was reality, and it forced the hard questions to light almost as much as Sullivan had in playing the loyalty card.

Why now? Why had Morgan approached him? Was it as simple as a thank you for helping her deal with her past, or was there more to it? Was it planned to use him as a tool from the beginning or was it simply a way for Metcalf to find out his feelings about her and the department?

Had she played him for a fool at the expense of his marriage? At the cost of the life he built? All in service of the department.

Resentment swelled and he found his answer in it. "I'm with you."

Sullivan squeezed his compatriot's shoulder. "Good. We have much to do to make things right at the DSA."

CHAPTER ELEVEN

His grin grew upon closing the Operations door. Soft mutterings wafted from beneath the frame, the collective frustration of Zac Modine joined the symphony of Sullivan's musings as he departed.

Everything was proceeding on schedule.

Three months of careful planning, of subtle manipulations, and finally the light was beginning to glow at the end of the tunnel. With each tug, each small nuanced threat introduced to those around him, Sullivan managed to tear apart the delicate ecosystem established by Metcalf over the course of the last decade. Once a cohesive force in the aid of her sister agencies, now the DSA appeared more akin to a high school drama club meeting: overwhelmed by emotion over logic.

Careful to maintain a lock on the joy threatening to slip from his curled lips, Sullivan started up the stairs and through the research hub for his waiting office. Those around him continued to operate at peak condition. Analysts paused to offer a wave when he passed, and he did the same. The cost to him was negligible, but he gained much from the simple exercise. It was a lesson that had never been learned by his superior. He shoved it in her face with each passing day.

He needed them all—from the lowliest of the support staff to the members of the field team still in play. Each performed a role in the upcoming play; each maintained a part in the performance to come. Sullivan's mission. His agenda.

He needed Zac most of all. The smile threatened to crack his cheeks in two. Sullivan was jubilant at the anguish left in Operations. Zac's night with Morgan had arrived at the perfect time, his feelings for the woman apparent the moment they'd returned from their time in Chicago. To act on them though? Sullivan had not believed the tepid tech possible of such an act. Zac's self-recriminations made it clear he paid for the decision.

Claire's call was timed to perfection as well. It was another divide, another chink in the department's cleverly crafted armor—another broken loyalty. All were being steered toward Sullivan and his goals. Zac was the crux of it, the reason for the constant attention—the need for his services too great to discount. The naive fool held the key to making it all work out in Sullivan's favor.

One way or another Zac would follow through.

Sullivan left the warm glow of the researchers, promises of coffee breaks and meals to come delivered, and rounded the corner for his office. His time approached faster than he'd believed possible. Every pawn was positioned, every scenario extrapolated and explored. It was time to push them forward.

It was time to find the Wellspring.

His hand fell on the office door, but then he paused. Sullivan sighed, hesitant to continue. He hated the room—hated the entire building, actually, but no place more so than the dreary windowless office. It was as cold as a tomb. The vents failed to operate despite the winter temperatures outside. He considered it little more than a prison cell, damning him upon entry time and again. Still, he entered, fighting through his dismal thoughts. The work was too important and almost at an end.

His every thought fell away at the sight of the man waiting inside. "Donald?"

"It's about time," Stallworth declared. He pushed through Sullivan's greeting to grab the open door. It slammed shut, echoing in the frame. Pudgy fingers turned the lock, clicking it into place.

The frantic Assistant Director of the NSA paced through the small space, leaving a wary Sullivan in his wake. Sweat dripped along graying temples and down his thick neck. Sullivan delivered his belongings to his desk, noting the emptiness on his daily calendar.

"I wasn't aware we had a meeting this morning," Sullivan said. "I certainly would have chosen a better venue."

Stallworth grumbled, hands clasped at his back. "Hollis

stopped by my office."

"He does get around, that one."

Stallworth's eyes thinned. "It wasn't a social visit, Greg. Nor a damn joke."

"What did he want, then?" Sullivan asked, feigning interest.

Stallworth joined him at the desk, leaning along the edge. "Questions are being asked. About our assessment hearing, and about our inquiries into this department."

Questions were understandable. Questions meant people were paying attention to events, those presented to them at least, not at those hidden from the spectacle of government work. Questions also came with answers, the more curious side of the equation in Sullivan's view.

"And what answers did you provide our good friend Mr. Hollis?"

It had only been three months since Sullivan's appointment, one which had come at Stallworth's insistence. It was meant to bring the burly man comfort and ease. Instead, the pressure of their work had begun to show on Stallworth. Calls arrived nightly to ask for updates from Sullivan. Progress reports were unnecessarily demanded. All requests were merely manifestations of Stallworth's feelings of guilt at maintaining the secrets behind their work.

"Nothing of consequence," Stallworth replied, his gaze lost to the shadows. "Routine proceedings. Standard follow-ups."

"Good," Sullivan said, rounding the desk. He remained standing, hands resting along the edge of the tabletop. "The problem, then?"

"You don't see it, do you," Stallworth pressed, agitation growing with each word. "Hollis? The Trust? If the question is asked they already hold the answer. They know what we're doing."

"That's fear talking, Donald," Sullivan answered, leaning toward his strained colleague. "Paranoia where there should be none."

They had kept the circle closed for that very reason. All vital information passed directly between them to minimize the chance of leaks or a paper trail. Those days would soon end. Progression required others to join their cause. It had to in order to gather the resources they required.

The Trust knew nothing. Sullivan chuckled at the very notion. For all its supposed power, they were slaves to their own systems. They asked passive questions—their method with everything.

At the sound of his companion's laughter, Stallworth huffed. His pacing resumed, the leather soles of his shoes squeaking incessantly with each lap.

"I was a fool to go along with this," he whined. "When you approached me with this endeavor after learning the truth behind the group I thought—"

"You thought you deserved something in return for your years of service. Something beyond the pittance handed your way thanks to the Trust's efforts."

Stallworth stopped. He straightened his tie and dabbed the sweat along his brow. "Yes. As I said. I was a fool. The DSA has served its purpose, unaware, for years."

Irritation crept in the deputy director's voice. His knuckles blanched white along the desk. "You put me here to keep it that way. We're so close, Donald. Metcalf knows. All we—"

Stallworth shook his head. "The Trust controls the Wellspring, Greg. They've used it for decades."

"To what end?" Sullivan shouted. He left the confines of the desk, cutting off Stallworth mid-lap. "The Trust, your ignorant puppet masters, are blind to the pain they cause by withholding miracles. Miracles we can share with the world."

"You play it off like you're some philanthropist, Greg," Stallworth said. "This isn't about a gift for humanity. This is about you getting the recognition you've always craved."

"It's what I deserve!" Sullivan rushed the man, surprise filling Stallworth's eyes. Greg's hands snatched the drenched collar of Stallworth's shirt and pinned him to the nearest wall. Fury ripped through the deputy director's body, rage in his every word. "I put everything on the line when I started out, believing it to be the right thing to do. The press, the American people, turned me into a joke. My own government shunned me. It took a lifetime to come back, clawing for any shred of self-respect, while I built a legacy."

He forced a breath, then released the man's collar and stepped away. Sullivan returned to the safety of his desk, allowing his calm and collected nature to reassert itself. Control returned, one that had served him well through the years. It had helped him reclaim his life after his fall from grace, to find a new path to his dreams.

Stallworth cleared his throat, rubbing his swollen neck. "That might be what this is, Greg. If the Trust find out the truth about your appointment here at the DSA and about what we're looking to take from them, we're dead men."

Sullivan sat, pulling his chair tight to the desk. He clasped his hands before him. The pawns were positioned, and the table was set for his well-conceived plans. The Trust were an obstacle and nothing more. He'd planned things out too well to let anyone stop him now.

"The pieces are almost in place, Donald," Sullivan said, darkness filling his wide eyes. "The Wellspring will be mine. *Then* everything will change. You'll see. Everyone will see."

CHAPTER TWELVE

The car glided to a halt on the solemn street. The rental hugged the curb before a lone brick building, a converted warehouse of days long since gone. A giant planet logo was perched atop the roof in large print, and the sign over the door read Big World Comics. Cal put the car in park and settled against the seat. Ben had allowed his new colleague to take the wheel rather than fight over the right to drive. He'd played that game enough over the last six weeks. There was also the slight embarrassment over not owning a car yet, which he preferred not to mention on top of everything else.

Morning rush hour had greeted them when they departed from the Edgemont, and the trek to Cordell Avenue had taken an exceptionally long time, mostly spent staring at the back side of every SUV and truck in the DC Metro area. Thankfully, Cal had kept the conversation going to distract Ben while they inched along the Dwight D. Eisenhower Memorial Highway. Ben had remained silent during the tutorial offered by the young attorney.

Ghosts, it seemed, came with their own hierarchy. The spirit realm maintained a class system of its own, ranging from the happy-pappy ghostly bunch all the way to the scary-ass nether creatures only the movie industry could reflect on the big screen. There was more to it, more levels and intricacies than Cal was willing to thrust upon the overwhelmed agent of the DSA, but the broad-strokes approach brought him up to speed.

Straight-up, plain-Jane—if you could call them that—ghosts were the Caspers of the bunch. Wanderers, aimlessly scattered throughout the world, unable to connect with those remaining.

They held no purpose, no redressing to consider after their end, but they stayed nonetheless out of fear of what came next.

Vengeful spirits—not a clever heavy metal band name—were able to affect the material world. Their power came from rage, though it presented itself more like an outburst than a controlled effect. Revenge cases were plentiful, but they remained easier to handle, as the target typically knew who they had pissed off. It was personal but also not life threatening.

That was where specters came into play. Revenge didn't even touch the anger behind their actions. Everything was personal to them, and they had more power, more control, to manipulate the material world and those living in it. They were task-oriented, not letting anyone or anything stand in their way.

Ben stopped him, not wanting to hear more. Not for a while, anyway. Creatures in the closet, viruses, cancers—bullets, even—concerned Ben. Believing the dead could play a part in his demise because of a swirly he gave back in grade school went beyond what he was willing to accept. Deep-seated doubts plagued him, the terrors of his childhood swallowed down rather than aired with the newfound colleague at his side. Ghosts weren't real, no matter *what* Cal believed. They couldn't be, could they?

If not, though, why continue the charade? Ben held his tongue and buried his doubts, willing to wait and see just where the investigation took them. However, he drew the line at welcoming the nightmares of his youth to the table. There had to be another explanation waiting for him. He simply had to find it.

"What are we doing here, again?" Ben tucked his hands deep into his pockets, and rushed across the street to the building in question. Cal patiently crossed at the corner with the signal. His path to the shop was irregular along the empty sidewalk—empty to Ben's eyes, at any rate. Cal tucked close, twisting and turning as if surrounded by hundreds of pedestrians during lunch hour. When he arrived at the shop a long trail of steam lifted from his lips, clearly relieved after the short walk. Ben, however, waited for more—confused by their arrival at the closed comic book store.

Cal pointed at the door. "We're seeing if Winslow was an isolated incident or if other victims have popped up," he said. "To see if anyone else might be connected and give us a starting point."

Ben scratched his head in response.

Cal sighed. "Weren't you the one that said that was the smart play?"

"Oh, I did," Ben replied, hopping up and down to build up heat against the cold of the morning. "Smart plays are my forte."

"I believe it," Cal muttered without looking. His eyes stayed on the small glyph marking the brick beside the handle of the front door. It looked like an hourglass to Ben. The lawyer's gloveless hand brushed against it.

The waiting agent cleared his throat. "What I mean by my very logical question is, why are we *here* for this information?"

"It's not just a comic book store."

Ben shook his head, moving for the picture window along the front of the establishment. He cupped his hands over his eyes to look within the darkened business. Rows of cardboard boxes lined the walls. Long folding tables were filled with books. Four bookshelves interspersed throughout the shop displayed colorful spines from hundreds of periodicals begging to be read.

Ben fell back on his heels away from the window and pointed inside. "I swear if there is a *Magic Cards* display I'm walking away from this whole thing."

Cal's head tilted to the right and his brow creased. "People tell you they don't understand your references, don't they?"

"All the time," Ben admitted with a grin.

"Just checking."

Ben reached for the handle, but it refused to turn under his grip. "The place is closed, Cal."

"Not to me." Cal reached into his pocket and retrieved a small key. Black with jagged teeth at the end and a rounded handle, it held no markings along the side. Cal slipped the instrument into the lock and it turned easily, a sharp click answering Ben's intended query.

"Why—?"

Cal pointed to the hourglass image near the door. "The hourglass represents time. Time and death aren't exactly bosom buddies, but they coincide all the same. This shop is one of an extensive network used throughout the world. A 'place for the dead' is a loose translation."

He opened the door for Ben, who reluctantly took hold, muttering, "Not creepy at all."

"Definitely creepy," Cal said, his voice a whisper. The door closed behind them after they stepped into the cozier atmosphere of the shop. Neither reached for the lights. "The symbol is also a sign to someone like me that the locks match the others."

"And you just happen to have a key?"

"Christmas present." Cal held the key before him. "Not from my wish list."

"I assume there's a story involved."

"Oh yeah," Cal said with a wry grin. "Dickens has nothing on me."

Footsteps behind them caused both men to spin on their heels toward the sound. Stepping out from a spiral stairwell to the apartment above, a chubby man in a *Ghost Rider* t-shirt approached cautiously. His right hand wielded a replica of Thor's hammer. *He must be worthy*, Ben thought, fighting the urge to grab his sidearm nestled tight at his hip.

"What the hell are you doing?" The middle-aged owner of the shop bellowed from the darkness of the stairs.

His answer came at the sight of the small key in Cal's hand.

"Oh. Figures." The man clicked the light switch behind him. The store remained in darkness, but their destination was illuminated with an over-sized *Eye of Agamotto* light fixture over a series of creaky steps leading to the basement. "Lock up when you're done."

The owner left without another word. Cal took the invitation, and graciously moved for the gold-encrusted eyeball guiding their way. Ben held back, hesitant to continue. The agent flipped through a stack of new releases with his back to his colleague.

"Coming?"

Ben tucked the books down on the table. He worked to straighten the pile, carefully shifting each side with precision until it was perfectly positioned. When that distraction failed, he reached for another. Cal tapped his foot on the carpet.

Ben smirked. "I'd rather not."

"Seriously?"

With a sigh, Ben followed the impatient attorney. The recently-cleaned atmosphere of the store with its colorful displays and incredibly articulate props lessened with each step toward the lower level of the shop. The room became drab, and the walls were covered in chipped off-white paint—though that was min-imal as most of the space was covered in bookcases. The shelves closest to the base of the steps contained overstock for the shop above, but as the pair shifted deeper into the basement the con-tents of the shelves became nothing but leather-bound editions, worn from age.

Not months or years either. They were dated decades earlier and longer. Each one was made of the same material. All the same size and depth, they ran the length of hundreds of shelves that lined the space from each wall, creating aisles like a library. Ben moved to reach for one dated February 1956, but Cal slapped it away, shaking his head before continuing toward the center of the room.

Ben tucked his hand in his pocket, his voice a whisper as he said, "So what are these places for the dead?"

"Repositories," Cal said. "Pretty much a giant spreadsheet, location specific, tracking the dying and the dead. Everyone that crosses the veil is identified and the information—name, date, time, and cause, if known—are noted in one of these books."

"But Winslow never crossed."

Cal took a deep breath. "Not completely. She did die, though. So her name should be listed, but not every detail of the event."

"Okay," Ben said with a shrug, unconvinced. "Who notes it in the book?"

Cal stopped at the center aisle that ran the length of the room. At the end was a thin door leading to a smaller space, where a lectern was positioned in the center. A book similar to the rest sat on top, opened to the middle.

"He does." Cal pointed toward the singular stand. Ben tracked his colleague's direction. At first nothing happened, then through the dim lighting of the basement Ben noticed the pen hanging in midair. His eyes widened when the page of the book resting on the lectern turned, as if a stiff wind had caught it.

"How?" Ben started to move for the small room, held back firmly by Cal.

"Reaper," the man said. Cal caught Ben's startled look and shook his head. "Not the one you're thinking. Sort of, though. A bookkeeper. Low-level staffer."

"Death as a corporation. Great."

"It is, unfortunately. I should handle this. These guys can

get… a little cranky."

"Reaper? Very dangerous. You go first." Ben ushered him toward the lectern. Cal remained stationary in the center aisle of the basement. Ben threw his hands in the air. "I know. Another reference."

"Oh, I got that one," Cal said, a thin grin spreading from his lips. "I would stay right there."

"Why?" Ben asked, suddenly nervous. "Cal?"

"One minute," Cal whispered as he made his way across the room. Ben struggled to stay still, unsure what the lawyer with the special vision had failed to tell him about reapers. Unsure whether to believe the man's word and break down in tears, or rush after him to demand the truth.

The overwhelmed ex-cop cursed his ceaseless doubts. "I don't like this crap."

Ben stuck close to the center aisle, focusing on the scene unfolding in the back room. Cal conversed with what appeared to be thin air before stepping in front of the book on the lectern. Ben couldn't help but wonder what was being said. Was he a fool for following Cal this far? What if it was all true; were the dead still part of the living world? Were there social graces to consider when approaching a reaper? A special handshake, perhaps? A bribe to make? Souls to offer?

Slowly, Cal returned. His head was low, and his eyes shifted around the room, lost in thought. "Well?" Ben pointed to the book. "Any other names?"

"None that fit our crime scene," Cal replied. He took the lead, heading for the steps.

"So Winslow was targeted specifically."

"Yes and no."

Ben stopped at the base of the stairs. He waited until Cal was almost to the top before calling him back, his patience for the guessing game long since passed. "Cal."

The young man paused. He sat on the step and ran his right hand through his hair. The messy strands fell over his forehead and he forced it back with his left. His eyes remained in motion, working something out behind the scenes.

"Sorry," he finally said. "There *was* a name listed."

"Winslow's," Ben said. "We knew that."

"No," Cal said, his eyes full of the same confusion as his companion. "It didn't read Abigail Winslow. It read Abigail Hunt."

CHAPTER THIRTEEN

Zac rubbed his hands together and continued to pace the sidewalk next to the intersection at Sixth and Frederick. His breath rose in thin streams. His lips moved while he paced. Constant grumblings grew with each lap.

Ben couldn't hear the words spoken. He rested comfortably in Cal's rental car. The heat blasted in the cabin as he studied the frustrated movements of his colleague. Zac had arrived ten minutes earlier, alone with a file containing the information Ben had requested.

The call was ill-advised but necessary. No matter his distrust of the situation at the DSA, Ben held no knowledge of Abigail Winslow or her former identity, recently gleaned by an invisible bookkeeper in the basement of a comic shop.

Just another reason why I stopped collecting...

Learning all they could about Abigail Hunt was the logical next step. Ben required it after following Cal's lead all morning. He needed something concrete, something substantial, and cemented in reality. Unfortunately his resources were limited, leaving him with only the frozen popsicle of an analyst for support.

"That's your guy, isn't it?" Cal asked. Concern rested in his voice as he tracked Ben's gaze to the only other individual intent on circling the same street corner for minutes on end. Midday traffic came and went, pedestrians moving in great strides. Ben, however, had picked the corner in particular for the slow periods. He needed to make sure Zac was alone, to find some level of trust before stepping into the cold.

"It is."

"Then why are we—?"

"It's nothing," Ben interjected. He reached for the handle. "I'll talk to him."

"Ben? I can—"

Ben smiled as the rush of cold slammed against his cheeks. "I've got it. Be right back."

The separation was another necessity. Fear drove his every action and he tired of it. He tired of the doubt resting with the DSA, as well as with the case of the dead agent laid at his feet.

Zac groaned when he caught sight of Ben approaching from the sedan. "Are you kidding me? Have you been here the whole time?"

Ben joined him at the corner. "Pretty much."

"I'm freezing my ass off."

"You're welcome," Ben replied. "Happy to help with the weight loss."

"I don't know why I bothered to come," Zac said, shaking his head. He started for his waiting car.

"Come on, Zac," Ben called. "At least leave the information."

"Such an ass," the tech groaned. He took a sharp breath and faced his colleague once more, extending out the file kept tight to his side. "Want to at least tell me what this is about?"

"If I say no, do I get the pouty face again?" Ben flipped through the paperwork. Personal records of Abigail Hunt, ending seven years ago. Right when the Winslow identity had come into being. Names, dates, cases, and known associates. Zac had come through. Ben peered up at the expecting tech. "She's dead."

"This is a case?"

Ben's gaze fell. "Sort of. Look, I don't expect you to understand, but I was hoping you could forget about this whole thing."

"I can't do that, Riley. There are protocols and procedures. If this is an open case, Operations needs to be briefed, agents tasked and coordinated with local assets. You know the drill."

"I do. I honestly and begrudgingly do, Zac." Ben tucked the file into his jacket, then jammed his hands into his pockets to bring some warmth back. "She died on my watch and I want to find her killer. Not play bureaucrat or whatever the hell I am when I'm at work. Do you know what I mean?"

Zac's eyes thinned. "Have you spoken to Morgan at all?"

"Huh? No, why?" Zac remained silent. Ben pressed with growing concern. "What's going on, Zac? Is she all right? Did something happen to her?"

"I… it's… she's fine," Zac stammered. "I just wanted to—"

"You sure?"

Zac nodded, unable to meet Ben's gaze. "Yeah. It's nothing. But Sullivan is going to want to know your status."

"And I will tell Sullivan everything when this is over. And Metcalf."

"Who was she?" Zac pressed. "Everything I found on this Hunt woman ends years ago. She was some deep cover agent for the FBI. Why did she turn up now?"

"That's what I'm trying to figure out."

Zac pointed to the waiting car, the figure in the driver-side window finally attracting enough attention for the tech to notice. "Who's your friend?"

"Witness to the crime."

"Then you should know your killer already."

"One would think," Ben said. "I appreciate your help, Zac. And your discretion?"

Zac hesitated. "Riley—"

"I wouldn't ask if it wasn't important. I'll understand if you have to file a report or whatever the hell it is you do when you blow me in."

"Really winning me over, Riley." Zac lifted the sleeve from his wrist to check his watch. "Twenty-four hours."

"Done and done." Ben held out his hand and Zac gave it a hard shake. File locked under his arm, he started back to the car.

"Riley," Zac said. "Is there something going on at the DSA I don't know about? Is everything okay with you at work?"

Ben returned, balancing on the steep curb. "I wish I knew, buddy."

"Yeah. Me too."

"What's wrong, Zac?"

Zac shook his head. "Doesn't matter. Go find your killer. Let me know if you need anything else."

"Thanks." Ben rushed to beat the change of the traffic signal. He left his colleague to the solitude of the corner. Ben opened the door and slipped inside, the heat washing over him like a blanket. He placed the file on his lap and patted it softly.

"That what we need?" Cal said. He waved to the hesitant tech. Ben did the same, grateful for the support. Zac eventually returned the gesture before heading back to his waiting car. There was something in his eyes, a heavy sadness about the day. Ben had no time to look into it now, however. They had the information they needed and a place to start.

Ben pointed to the open road. The traffic light changed to green for them as if on cue. "Let's go find out who Abigail Hunt really was."

CHAPTER FOURTEEN

Every step was riddled with hesitation for Morgan. Every movement, every action, brought with it a pang of anger followed by a trail of guilt. Questions and doubts about the validity of her assignment grew even as she reached the door to Lincoln's apartment.

The soft click of the lock met with a loud creak when the door finally slid open. Morgan paused, letting the key fall back into the pocket. She'd earned it over time. It had been a long road with Lincoln, one that had started upon her arrival. Her own distance from people had kept things from progressing, but his strength had impassioned her to spark a friendship. She was grateful he had accepted at the time—trusting her with something as personal as a key to his apartment. Now, however, she wished she had never made the approach.

She hated being here: in his place, the one private location afforded a field agent of the DSA. They came to the department broken pieces willing to do the work. Every action they took was scrutinized, their backgrounds rehashed at the convenience of anyone and everyone, from Metcalf up to the Council at the top of the food chain. Their lives were no longer their own. They answered for every thought, every edict, every misstep, and every betrayal. Their homes, however—while government issued—were their own.

Her invitation to Zac was the first she had ever made. She wondered if Lincoln had kept his guest list to a minimum as well—possibly only to Ruth Heller.

Ruth. It came back to Bellbrook and always would. Bellbrook. The Witness. Even the science behind the signal brought on by a dead doctor: Howard Clevinger. Every detail was ingrained in their thinking, every act an attempt to move past the events of that night while also seeking justice for the lives lost.

Morgan took it that way, anyway. Lincoln's actions in Des Moines gave her a different impression—one that concerned her greatly. Two dead men, both with military backgrounds, made things more complicated. The situation showed Morgan how far gone Lincoln truly was.

I'll find him.

That was her vow to Metcalf; her promise to resolve the growing conflict occurring in the background of the DSA. But should she? Was bringing Lincoln back the right move? She definitely couldn't let him go without question—the dead men saw to that. There must have been something else to it, something deeper she couldn't see. More questions needed answering. She hoped those answers would give her some clue as to how to handle Lincoln. How to help him.

She cursed upon entering the apartment. The entire situation could have been avoided had she answered her phone. It did not matter that she had been hundreds of miles away facing certain death at the hands of a black ops team in Chicago. She should have been there for him. They were colleagues and they were friends.

Lincoln needed help. That much was clear. Morgan had to be there for him, missed opportunities or not.

The apartment was dark, the curtains throughout drawn. It did not keep the dust at bay. Thick layers ran along the minimal amount of furniture kept in the one bedroom at Westwood Tower. Cleaning must not have been high on Lincoln's priority list. The garbage in the kitchen was emptied, no liner in the can at all. The fridge held little more than beer and cold cuts.

At first glance, the living room appeared every bit as impersonal as Lincoln presented himself at work. There was minimal furniture throughout the place, and nothing on the walls. Hidden in the corner, beside a recliner, rested a small bookshelf filled to bursting. A record player sat on top, the accompanying music organized meticulously beneath. Vinyl, not the modern equivalent. Where the couch appeared new, the chair's cushion settled along the wood frame at its base, and the arms were worn from use.

Morgan had never known about his love of music. She had never known anything more about Lincoln than the bullet-producing, action-movie-watching alpha male he offered at the workplace. She smiled at the thought of him sitting in the darkness of the apartment, a beer in hand and Miles Davis booming in his ears.

The smile faded just as quickly as she remembered her purpose for the visit. Not to reconnect, but to locate. Not to cherish, but to interrogate.

The desk in the bedroom was empty and more dust littered the tabletop. It surrounded the few books positioned against the wall, held tight by plastic bookends. There were artillery records from past conflicts overseas and historical documents pertaining to troop deployments. There were dozens of accounts from the bloodiest war zones in history. He was always the soldier. Why that suddenly worried Morgan as much as it did, she couldn't say, but she put the thought aside to finish her sweep of the apartment.

There was nothing. No trace of the man, no reason to believe he had returned for a spell. Frustrated, Morgan returned to the front door. Her hand squeezed the knob. This was his world, all he had left, all *any* of them truly owned outside of the work. To lose that sanctuary, what would it do to her? What had it done to Lincoln?

She closed the door behind her, securing the bolt firmly in place to keep out any visitors to the private sanctuary. Lincoln wasn't coming back, and any thought to the contrary was a lost effort. Frustrated at the wasted time and without a clue where to continue, Morgan returned to the street and the bitter breeze ripping down the block.

Winter needed to end, her preference for the warmth of summer spiking with each step into the cold. She should have worn a warmer hat or two, possibly a second set of gloves as well. The season never suited her and only left her empty, despite the warmth of the morning with Zac.

Her phone chirped in her pocket, and a hopeful smile formed on her lips. Was he calling her? Did Zac miss her after only a few hours apart? The word RESTRICTED was emblazoned on the display. She accepted the call, the phone tucked under the flap of her hat so she could hear.

A deep voice filled her ear, and her eyes widened. "You didn't mess up my album collection, did you?"

"Lincoln?" She scanned the block while backing closer to the building for a better view. Pedestrians mingled outside a consignment shop at the opposite corner of the intersection. Others rushed to their cars, trying to beat the clock with little chance of success. The idle vehicles appeared empty. The windows of the apartment buildings across the way were all darkened by shades or the shadows of the morning. She continued to peer around for some sign of life, her glove tight to the phone as if trying to reach through for him.

"We need to talk, Linc."

"I know," he replied, the words as cold as the wind. "Not here."

"Don't play this game," she said. "We need—"

"No game," Lincoln said, cutting her off. "I'll text you the address. Midnight. Come alone."

"Lincoln, don't—"

"See you then, Morgan. And get yourself a warmer coat. It's freezing out."

The line went dead, the click echoing in her ear. She removed the phone and put it away. Her eyes never left the street. Cars continued to filter in and out of traffic. Passersby shot her looks of confusion, yet returned to their own conversation in time. She detected no outward sign of his presence. Lincoln controlled the situation.

It worried her to no end. Especially as her phone chimed again, the text message with the location received. It was going to be a long day.

"Great."

CHAPTER FIFTEEN

Megan Daniels lived alone. A modest Cape Cod along Westlake Drive, the Daniels' home had stepped out of a brighter past with painted shutters along the front windows and a welcome mat at the front door recently freed from the piling-up overnight snow. The interior maintained the illusion of better days. A fireplace in the living room warmed the first floor. Photos in spotless frames hung around the mantel. Even the kitchen held a rustic charm, with small candles burning above the sink as well as aprons hanging in the corner over the winter boots and coat near the rear entrance.

Ben relaxed in the creaking oak chair of the kitchen table nestled in the corner of the narrow room. The midday sun caught the pristine white curtains of the window beside him, lighting up the entire room and beyond. In the family room Cal's soft footfalls paced slowly along the carpet in front of the mantel.

"What is this about, again?" Megan sat across from Ben at the small, round kitchen table. Nursing a cup of coffee, the middle-age woman with thin blond locks checked the wall clock for the time. She had been quick to note it was her lunch hour from work. Even working from home for a telecommunications firm meant keeping track of the clock in case a supervisor noted her station idling, or a potential client reached out with issues.

The question that came with his visit was one Ben had considered all morning. Since their stop at the place of the dead he had wondered more and more about the woman known as Abigail Winslow. The woman the bookkeepers from beyond the veil had labeled with the surname Hunt. Why had she changed her name and how had the DSA missed something like that when hiring her?

From there, the logical extension was why join the DSA at all? Of all the places for her to end up, why there? And why the same apartment building as their other recent recruit? Her apartment had had a full view of his own across the way and was filled with surveillance equipment to monitor his every action. But under whose orders? Metcalf or Sullivan? The eternal choice between his two superiors weighed on him, yet offered nothing but questions.

Cal shared the same conclusion. Ben noticed the mixed look of frustration and concern on the lawyer's face. His shoes threatened to wear down the carpet from his pacing. Cal believed he was getting closer to answers with his family, instead of wading deeper into a new mystery.

Ben smiled disarmingly at the woman across the table. "Like I said, Mrs. Daniels, it's about Abigail Hunt."

Megan fiddled with the thin gold chain dangling from her neck at the mention of the name. A plastic ring was looped around the necklace, a pink butterfly charm on the face. Her eyes remained fixated on the cup of coffee in front of her. The dossier obtained offered up the connection between Hunt and the Daniels family. He was glad that Zac appeared thoroughly distracted during their chat. He hadn't made the first-name connection with their new recruit. Zac's quick work had tracked down everything available in their archives as well as the FBI's personnel files offering Ben a picture of their victim.

It was the only place to start. There was still no indication of motive in the crime, if such a thing existed when speaking of the dead. So far, though, they had come up empty. Hunt was an agent with the FBI, but her record was clean. *Appeared* to be clean, anyway. Reports were redacted or simply lost. Case files had been mismanaged. Only a list of Hunt's colleagues was noted for their review. Two former supervisors had given them little to go on, offering barely more than five minutes of their time before shuffling them to the door. The wife of Steven Daniels topped the list of potentials for their next visit. The rental car sped through the bustling streets of Bethesda for the Cape Cod home along Westlake.

"What? Is she okay?" Megan asked at hearing the name of her husband's former partner.

Ben's eyes softened. "I'm sorry to have to tell you this. We found her body this morning."

"She's dead?" The question was barely audible. Megan shifted to the single photo attached to the front of the refrigerator. Ben recognized a younger Megan, one not sporting the thin lines running from her eyes or the puffy cheeks. The lithe, muscular gentleman beside her must have been her husband. Steven Daniels had been an agent with the Federal Bureau of Investigation for twelve years before his untimely death. His presence was everywhere in the home, despite his absence. The coat and boots were his, much too large for the woman seated across from him. Books lined the mantel, historical accounts and true crime being the genres of choice compared to the shelves of early twentieth-century poetry on the other side of the room. It was as if he was still in the room with the widow. Megan shook her head, turning back to Ben with tears welling in her blue eyes. "Did some-one...?"

"We're looking into that," Ben replied. The less she thought about it, the better. "We understand she was partners with your late husband, Steven?"

"That's right." Her fingers returned to the charm along her neck. She dropped it when she caught Ben watching. Moving to stand, Megan pointed to the fridge. "I'm sorry, would you like something to drink? There are also some leftovers if you're hun-gry?"

"We're fine," Ben said, waving her back. Both peered into the family room and the silent third member of their conversation. Cal smirked and nodded his acceptance of Ben's decision. Me-gan settled on her chair, hand to her neck and touching the wait-ing charm. "I'm sorry. Is that a butterfly?"

She smiled, removing the charm from the chain. "From our first date. One of those stupid quarter games at the local fair. I always keep it near me."

"It's a lovely memento," Ben whispered. He ran a finger along his tie. "Now, about Agent Hunt?"

"Right." She clicked the object back into place. Her hands wrapped snugly around her coffee cup. "They were partners at the Bureau. I think for about four years or so? That was when..."

Ben reached for her hand, his voice soft as he said, "When you lost your husband."

"She would visit occasionally. Have dinner here. Mostly work talk. It was like they didn't have anything else in their lives."

The notion hit Ben harder than he would have liked. He swallowed his selfish thoughts, returning to the widow. "They did a lot of undercover work?"

"I don't have many details except what... what they told me after."

"Your husband was killed in the line of duty?" Ben asked, though he hated to. Megan's comfort level dropped. Her body shifted along the creaking chair and her hand retreated to her chest, fighting the urge to return to her necklace.

"Yes," she answered. She took a long sip of her coffee. "A, what do you call them? A sting gone bad. Somebody messed up their cover before they could catch whoever they were after."

Ben nodded, recalling the details from the file. "I read the report. Your husband was caught in the middle. For some reason, Abigail wasn't there."

"No," she said loudly, her eyes wide. The volume of her reply seemed to frighten her and she forced herself to settle and take a breath. "They... they said she was late for the meeting. Traffic. Saved by a red light."

Cal stepped into the kitchen, surprising Ben for a moment. The young lawyer knelt beside the table. "We're sorry to have to bring all this up for you."

"I just miss him," she said, wiping her eyes. "It's okay."

Ben felt like a heel, continuing with his questions. Still, he proceeded, thoughts only on the killer — ghost or otherwise. "Did you ever talk to Abigail after it happened?"

"No." She kept her eyes on the thinning stream of heat rising from the cup. "I never saw her again."

"Not even at the funeral?"

"No," she said. "Steven had a lot of friends from work. They had so many nice things to say about him. So many memories. But I never saw her again. Never heard from her."

Cal pointed to the images along the mantel of the family room. "Did any of those friends ever share any stories about Abigail with you?"

"I'm sorry?" Megan said, a curious look on her face. The feeling matched Ben's, who wondered about Cal's motivations. Was he looking for a killer still, or had Cal shifted back to his own case? Had it always been about *his* family instead of the here and now?

Cal stood, then moved for the fridge. His fingers tapped lightly next to the image of Steven held up by a small bag clip magnet. "I know how office gossip gets around. Maybe his friends mentioned something to you? Something to help us figure out why someone would want to hurt Abigail?"

Or why she changed her name, Ben wanted to add.

"I don't..." Megan trailed off, refusing to look at either of them.

Cal returned to her side. He crouched to catch her gaze. "It would help us a lot, Mrs. Daniels."

Megan relented, shaking her head. "No."

"No?"

"No one ever said anything about her."

Ben and his companion shared an unsteady glance while Megan turned to check the clock once again. She focused on the soft ticking sound filling the silence.

Unwilling to press further, and seeing no need for more questions, Ben stood with a smile. "Thank you for your time, ma'am."

Surprise met him, her reaction to their sudden shuffling for the front door. She escorted them out, and the sadness faded from her face. As Ben and Cal retrieved their winter gear, long overcoats with thin leather gloves for both gentlemen, Megan held firm to the wall at the far end of the foyer near the base of the staircase to the second floor.

"Are you sure I can't get you anything?" she inquired, her words hesitant and distant; their welcome had long since passed.

"That's all right," Cal said while Ben finished gearing up for the trek outside.

"Yeah," Ben continued. "We have quite a few stops to make today."

"The work never ends. Steven said that all the time," Megan said. She stepped between them to open the front door. Cal led the way to push open the outer door to the wooden porch that stretched the length of the home. Ben followed, the wind attacking him immediately. Megan stood in the door frame to watch their departure. Her pale skin blended with the painted siding of the home.

"He was not wrong," Ben said. He took the steps two at a time to the stone walkway.

"He never was." Her words caught in the midday wind. Words lost to memories which refused to fade.

Ben stopped in the driveway, then turned back up the path. Reaching into his pocket he found a small index card and quickly jotted his number down on it. He held the makeshift business card out, and was grateful when she took it. "Call if you think of anything. Thanks."

Ben returned to the end of the driveway and his waiting companion. Rental keys dangled before Cal like a pendulum.

"Agent?" Megan called from the open door. Her eyes were small glass orbs of light. Frozen and cold. "Did she suffer at all?"

The questioned surprised Ben, who stuttered as he tried to find an answer. Cal stepped in front of him. "No," he said. "It was sudden. She didn't feel a thing."

Both men shuffled into the rental car. The sedan jerked into the slow flow of traffic. The salt on the streets crunched beneath tires, slush coating the underside as they sped along Westlake toward their next destination. Thick, black clouds rested along the horizon, inching closer to the city.

None of it mattered at the moment to Ben. His thoughts rested on the still-grieving widow in the rearview mirror — more importantly, the cold stare that had accompanied her final query. *Did she suffer at all?* The way they grew when she asked, begging for an answer.

Those eyes followed him the rest of the day.

CHAPTER SIXTEEN

"That was painful."

It was an understatement shared by Ben when he and Cal entered the seventh-floor apartment after an extremely long day. Both men shed their winter gear, tossing coats and gloves on the two chairs positioned at the small kitchen table. Ben rubbed the weariness from his eyes and headed straight for the refrigerator.

"That is putting it lightly," he said to Cal, who groaned. The lawyer's backside hit the couch in the center of the living room. Ben called from the open fridge, "Beer?"

"Please," Cal said, rubbing his swollen feet. "You do this for a living? I think my toes fell off at the sixth character witness."

Most cases involved witnesses of a different sort, with some viable information to share about their victim or killer. Despite the fourteen stops they had made, the amount of information gleaned about the past life of Abigail Winslow barely filled a single sheet of legal pad paper.

They had talked to former supervisors, partners, and colleagues that lost touch with the woman, presumably due to her change of identity. None knew more than what was on record. Most held only a cursory knowledge of the woman, having stuck to a professional level. Winslow had no actual friends, from what they gleaned. Deep-cover assignments always made personal relationships difficult. This, however, was something more. It was as if she intentionally cut herself off from humanity. It certainly complicated their investigation.

Ben sipped his beer, handing the other to Cal's waiting hand. The lid twisted off with a satisfying hiss, and he joined the toast to a wasted day. Ben sat in the recliner across from the couch in front of the mantel decorated with family photos—what few Metcalf's people had lifted from his apartment after his recruitment. "How do you find a killer when your victim has so much to hide?"

"Maybe your agency can help us a bit more. You guys hired her, right? Someone might have dug up the reason for the identity change."

It was a good thought. Still, Ben couldn't help but glance away. There were nearly a dozen messages waiting on his cell phone. Each one was from Metcalf. Her questioning voice rang in his ears, even without listening to a single word. No doubt she wanted him back at the office, where he could coordinate the case. Her way. She wouldn't say it directly. The edict was inherently implied.

Ben cursed silently. Zac's help was one thing, as the information was helpful without putting the tech in the line of fire. Anything more would have been dangerous, and he was already playing things close to the edge. There was a murder to consider, one of their own. That should have been priority one. If Cal was on the level, the DSA would recognize his gift. Metcalf included. She would have no choice. But Ben didn't call them, not since his meeting with Zac to procure Hunt's personnel file. He didn't use the resources at his disposal. He had only relied on Cal, the lawyer with a gift Ben fought to accept, to back him up.

Ben's eyes caught sight of the report centered on his otherwise cleared desk in the spare room. The Grissom File. Right now the DSA held too much baggage for him: Sullivan's threats, as well as Metcalf's lies and secrets. He was caught in the middle, manipulated on both ends. There was also Cal to consider. Ben's time in Chicago with a young man named Henry Reed had ended with the kid being carted away to a government facility for what was purported to be further study into his rare talent. Ben didn't want a repeat performance with the man sitting across from him.

Realizing Cal still awaited an answer, Ben slowly shook his head. The curious attorney leaned over the edge of the couch. "No good? That Zac guy seemed all right."

"He has his moments," Ben said, rubbing his neck. "No, it's not that. It is a smart idea, in fact. Work, though, isn't exactly the place I hoped it would be. There are questions I need answered and some that shouldn't be asked."

His words came off as whining, bitter at the second chance given. Cal took the explanation with a nod, glancing around the apartment for the first time since entering. Boxes littered the apartment, tucked in the corners of each room and filling the closets. The photos displayed on the mantel were the rare items that had been unpacked. Positioned in the middle was a framed photograph of Ben in uniform, standing with an older gentleman. The man at his side gave a hard stare through his horn-rimmed glasses.

"That the reason for living out of boxes?"

Ben sipped his beer. "No time."

"Or no reason to," Cal said.

Ben considered the notion. The boxes, all labeled neatly though not by his hand, had remained closed since his arrival to his new life in Bethesda with the DSA. They were pockets and pieces of a life he never wanted to lose back in Buffalo. His former life had been sifted through by strangers, each item carefully inspected by his new employer before being transported to the appointed living quarters. He had yet to do an inventory, let alone shop for what had been missed.

His thoughts were distant when he answered Cal, "Maybe."

"I get it," Cal said, his toes flexing along the thin carpet. "I've spent years hiding what was going on with me. I mean, it's a conversation stopper, to say the least. I want nothing to do with it."

"There's a difference, Cal."

"Not that I see."

"Look harder," Ben pressed. He finished the beer and placed the bottle at the side of the recliner. The blue eyes of his companion wavered over Ben's right shoulder and the images on the mantel—almost afraid to catch Ben's stare. "You can help people, Cal, living *and* dead. You can hear the pleas from people in pain and bring them the peace they deserve. You view it as a curse, but it isn't. Not unless you want it to be."

"You could say the same."

Ben shook his head. "I've tried trusting those I'm not sure earned it. I have. But I never wanted this life. This was his."

He turned back to the image of his father. Part of Ben remained in his father's shadow, forever buried under the weight of his expectations, even after his death. Every choice, the re-sponsibility, the path ahead, had all been drawn up by him and his needs. Never by Ben.

"Your dad?" Cal asked, staring to the right of his host.

"He's probably somewhere in the room, cursing me out for mentioning his name." Ben stood and circled the chair. He lifted the image and held it out. "Cal?"

"Hmm?" The attorney shook his head, rubbing his eyes. "No. I don't see anyone."

"I do," Ben muttered. "Every day. This is what he wanted. The only way to make a difference in his eyes. All I ever see is the darkness in it though. The pain and the misery that comes with each crime and with each death. Never the light."

"You're looking at it wrong," Cal said. "The job might be dark, but it was always going to be that way. You're the one bringing the light to it." Ben chuckled at the notion even as Cal's strong words echoed in the dimly lit room. "What's so funny about that? Okay, it might be a cheesy line. However, there is *some* validity to said cheesiness."

"It isn't that," Ben replied. Then he smiled. "Well, it is. Cheese or no cheese, it's you, Cal. How you go on after losing your family. It's incredible."

"You do the same," Cal said. He pointed to the image. "Buf-falo, right?"

"Born and raised."

"Yeah." Cal nodded. "I thought the name sounded familiar. I followed your case on the news. Even managed to read some of the testimony transcripts."

"Now, Cal—" Ben tried to find something to say, some way to dissuade the man's thinking. Cal caught the look and waved him off.

"Don't worry. Your secret is safe. Though I'm curious how the Nickel City's very own Judas-with-a-badge avoided jail time after that one-sided freak show called a trial."

Ben wasn't surprised at being found out. What kept him in-terested in the young attorney from Albany was how he man-aged to stay composed: the attitude, and the outlook, with every-thing that happened to him. Somehow, thanks to the time they had spent together Ben did know his secret was safe, and ulti-mately had another reason not to open the door to Metcalf and the rest of the DSA on this case.

"Job opportunity," he said with a shrug.

"That you hate."

There were things he could share, things from his time at the DSA that would shock the young attorney. Bellbrook. Chicago. As well as his personal dilemma with Sullivan and Metcalf. Cal's comment struck a nerve, because he was absolutely right. Ben just hadn't realized it until that moment.

"No," Ben admitted. "There's been days... some, not many, but some decent days. I don't know. I'm pretty far out of my element, you know?"

"Oh?" Cal exclaimed sarcastically. "I had no idea."

Ben pointed to the empty bottle in his colleague's hands. "Another?"

"No, I'm good." Cal wiped the remnants from his lips. "So where would you go if you left? What would you do?"

"Not a clue," Ben said distantly, his thoughts suddenly stuck on the missing Emily Wright. Another situation created by his recruitment to the DSA. Another question yet to be answered. She joined the Grissom File, the Witness, and so many others in the pile of unknowns mounted against him. "Can't even think about it. Not like I have any other options."

"That's where you're wrong. Everything is an option, including your time at the TSA or wherever the hell it is you work."

Ben laughed, relaxing into the recliner. "DSA."

Cal shook his head. "Horrible name. Just horrible. Anyway, this is something new. Something bigger and overwhelming at times. You see the burdens, the darkness in it. Why not take a second to focus on the good you bring to the table? The good you can do by staying?"

Ben smiled at the intensity behind Cal's every word. "I can see why you became an attorney. I bet you're damn good at it too."

"I am awful at it, in fact," Cal said. "I just refuse to give up the floor without a fight."

"I concede, Counselor." Ben stood, his hands raised in surrender. He collected the beer bottles, then moved for the empty sink to rinse them out.

"I should head back to my accommodations," Cal yawned, reaching for his coat.

"Couch is available."

Cal waved his hands. "I couldn't."

"Saves me the trouble of tracking you down in the morning for more legwork." Cal's face drooped at the idea of more interviews. Ben smiled, patting his back. Ben took the coat and let it fall back on the chair, ushering Cal over to the less-than-comfortable, yet suitable couch. "I mean, I know it's in an apartment—"

"It's perfect," Cal noted. "Hotels are much worse. Trust me. And thanks."

"Thank you."

Ben left his new colleague and started for his bedroom. Sleep would come quickly. Morning would arrive too soon as well. That was a fact of his new life. Just as it was a fact that the next day would bring more insight into the murderer they were tracking. It was bigger than him, just as everything else had become since joining the Department of Special Assignments, but Ben went to bed thinking about his world differently for the first time since leaving Buffalo.

Things seemed a little brighter to Ben, and he was less alone than he had ever realized.

CHAPTER SEVENTEEN

The destination was clear. Morgan took the short drive to Silver Spring and the auto junkyard that inhabited the entire block of Wetzler and Davis. Her sedan idled across the street while she looked over the site. It was a less-than-ideal location in the burgeoning suburb, and people roamed the streets aimlessly as the moon rose overhead in a thin curve of white lancing the darkness. The cloud-filled sky did little to hamper the deep chill settling into the area, the temperatures dropping steeply to match the snow during the late-night hours. Morgan could feel the cold through her thin, leather gloves and down coat.

She took the time to contact Metcalf. The director's answers were curt, frustrating her, especially considering the effort made that morning to give her the assignment. Saving Lincoln *was* the goal, wasn't it? Yet everything she heard on the line made it sound secondary to putting an end to an embarrassment for the department. Even the mention of the man's name was cut short or interrupted. Metcalf refused to lift another finger. She had played the only card available to her. It was up to Morgan to make the difference.

Lincoln wasn't making matters easy.

The tall woman hugged tight to what little body heat she carried from the car as she moved into the auto yard. With each step her concern grew. The distance maintained by Lincoln in setting up their meeting gave her the impression of a lack of trust. Lincoln had somehow known Metcalf would send her, and had still set up the meeting the way he did. A precaution? Possibly. Morgan held onto that singular hope, but deep down she knew Lincoln was changed from his time in Des Moines. Killing always changed people. No matter how many times the act was repeated.

The fence had been ripped away along the rear and a clear point of entry opened, despite the warnings of trespassing throughout the property. Looking closer, she realized the ends that had been sheared away were still sharp, not dulled or rusted from age. The cuts were new — likely Lincoln's doing.

She remained cautious upon entering. Her steps were deliberate as she moved through the fields of old clunkers and decaying scrap metal. The location also meant caution on Lincoln's part. She tried to stick with caution rather than its cousin term: paranoia. Paranoia was never good when taken in context with a retired military man like Lincoln. PTSD was the buzzword of the decade, but more than anything, guys trained to kill without thought were dangerous, particularly in a venue of their choosing with adequate prep time. Given enough time, dangerous became an understatement.

Morgan shared the background, though not to the same extent as Lincoln. She had been in hot spots, seen unspeakable evil on both sides of conflicts, and had come out with the same invisible scars as the rest of those who served. Those scars were the ones to worry about, tucked under the surface. They ate away at all the virtuous intentions and well-thought-out plans. They stripped men and women of their family and friends — of their very lives.

Lincoln had it worse. Morgan accepted that as simple fact. It didn't mean he couldn't be reached, if need be. She remained hopeful this would be a conversation and not a debate.

Hope slipped away when she entered into a small clearing at the center of the yard. Four large stacks of cars surrounded the site like pylons. Smaller obstacles blocked the pathways between the larger columns on three of the four sides. Tires had been positioned on one end, an abandoned vehicle at the other two — each high enough to keep her locked in the small area surrounded by debris and scrap. Morgan gripped her sidearm tighter, the realization of what she stepped into growing clear.

A kill box.

She recognized the configuration from her time in Afghanistan. The goal was to force a target to a specific destination, contain them, and then drop the hammer. Tactics 101 and she had fallen for it, too lost in her own head to worry about the world right in front of her the entire time.

Stopping in the center, Morgan lifted her Glock. Her finger left its position on the trigger, remaining visible to anyone watching her. She slowly spun in a circle. Her other hand opened her jacket, the cold ripping through her as she showed the lack of surveillance devices on her person. There was nothing to conceal, no play to be made. It wouldn't be enough, but it was a start.

Every conversation needed an opening. She hoped her faith in her colleague was justified.

"Paranoid, Lincoln?" she called out into the darkness. She remained in the center of the kill box, her question rising against the four columns surrounding her.

Behind her a soft click sounded—the catch on a sidearm disengaging the safety. Morgan spun around quickly and a shadow stepped into the light. A thin beard covered his cheeks. A coat and hat aided his efforts, tight to his muscular frame so as not to impede his movements. Lincoln's eyes blazed in the moonlight as he stepped into the box without a sound.

"Cautious, Morgan," he said. He kept his gun steady on her. "Very cautious."

CHAPTER EIGHTEEN

Excuses. It boiled down to excuses in Cal's mind. Memories of a phone call he wished he could repeat ran through his thoughts. He never should have answered it in the first place. He had meant to ignore the call, to send it straight to voicemail and pretend the message never made it to him—lost to the digital ether. He wanted to claim the entropic cell phone had devoured all trace of his mother's robotic voice and his father's concerned tone. When they called, he was busy. There was a girl involved and Cal put her above all else—even family.

They had made plans for the holidays, plans away from Albany and responsibility. His parents would never have understood. In their eyes Cal was duty-bound to attend as he had every year of his life. It was funny to hear them talk about things like duty and obligation though, considering they had barely known the meaning of the word since they fell into the American dream of money and privilege. Cal still recalled a time before that, when family meant something, when caring for each other through the hard times involved more than throwing a grand—or fifty—at the situation to resolve it. So when his mother had cooed in his ear for his attention and his attendance to their annual Christmas party, Cal had declined—vehemently.

Life with Lori was different from being with family. It was another excuse, but one that took hold in the moment of that phone call. She never judged him, never showed disappointment in starting at the bottom of the firm where he worked all hours of the night to help people with scarce funds make rent—even before he worried about them paying their legal fees. She never complained about the one-bedroom apartment he occupied in a small nook outside the city. He had chosen it for the quiet. There had been other reasons as well, though he refused to share them and she never pressed the issue.

She never cared to know, never had to live with that knowledge, with the burden of his secret. His so-called gift had labeled him an outcast and a lunatic all in the same breath.

His mother had sighed into the phone when he'd declined the invitation. She pleaded, of course, the attempt almost emotional, yet still held back by a wave of apathy. It had been his mother's go-to modus operandi since the accident, since his time away at the sanitarium under guarded observation.

His father had taken over, genuine concern in his voice. For all his failings, for all the distance between them, there was a respect he'd held for the old man, and his father returned it in kind. Questions of recent cases had quickly taken over the conversation. His father had even offered legal tactics to help Cal's clients. Now he wished his father had pushed harder, argued longer for his presence at the dinner.

It would be their last meal among the living.

Cal struggled with the knowledge of their demise, of being the sole survivor to the Cooper name. It followed him in his sleep, and he tossed and turned along the stiff cushion of the couch. The dreams held firm, refusing to allow him a breath.

They always started with the call, with Lori and her beauty in that last peaceful moment. When life had made sense and the future had been wide open. Then the screams took over.

His sister started the chorus, begging him for an answer—demanding to know who took her life. His brothers moaned in the background for justice, something lost the night the Coopers were massacred in their home. He knew the real reason for their screams: his family demanded his very sanity as payment for surviving.

After their deaths, Cal never again set foot in the home. He never visited the crime scene where his siblings, his parents, nieces, and nephews had shared their last conversations and their dying breaths together. The answer might have been there, but something else was as well. His guilt, his regret, at answering that fateful phone call.

Where were you, Cal?

"I was busy," Cal grumbled, his brow soaked from the

dream. His father shook his head, disappointment complete. Cal had tried to make the man proud, following in his footsteps through law school. He had taken a staffer job at the firm for a time as well, but it had never sat well with him. He'd left quickly for another job—one he had earned with his work, not his surname. "I'm sorry."

You should have been there.

You could have saved us!

Was it false hope or an outright lie that echoed through his dream, or had they simply been more excuses? The truth was he would have died, same as the others. Of that, Cal had no doubt. Not for an instant. Yet the nightmare persisted. The dream refused him one moment of peace in a lifetime of struggle.

"I'm sorry…"

Unceasing. Unending. Excuses and guilt.

"I'm sorry!"

He woke with a start, hand slamming against the coffee table for balance to keep his weary frame from collapsing onto the carpet beneath his makeshift bed.

The pair of blankets provided by his host were scattered at his feet, and the lamp of the end table dangled precariously along the edge. Cal wiped the sweat dripping through his hair, pushing the mess back and away from his tired eyes. He fixed the lamp, and then he sat at the end of the couch, hands clasped tight in his lap.

Even here, searching for some kind of answer, wasn't enough. He knew the house waited for him, begging him to enter to hear their final words, yet he resisted. The guilt from the call, the regret at not standing with the others as they met their maker, held him back.

Their disappointment was enough. He didn't need it to carry into the afterlife. Not for a second.

"I'm sorry," he muttered under his breath. His heart slowed; however, a thundering continued. Not from him, his wandering hands discovered as the thrumming rang out louder with each beat, but from behind him.

The bedroom.

"Ben?"

Cal jumped to his feet, and his knee slammed against the edge of the end table. His curse echoed in his ears, but went no farther; it was lost to the growing cacophony of the bedroom. Shadows danced beneath the frame of the door, a puzzled look building on the young attorney's face as he approached with clumsy steps.

"Ben?" he called once more. A soft rap on the door sent it sliding from its position near the frame. "Everything all right?"

Ben was not resting in his bed. He was not lost to the warm embrace of sleep from their long day on the hunt for a killer. He hovered in space above the welcoming mattress, hands on his throat as he struggled for breath.

Panic filled Ben's eyes. The terror came in the form of the killer among them; one completely unseen by the floating agent: the specter. Tendril-like fingers stole the air from Ben's lungs. Cavernous eyes of black flared with anticipation at the impending demise.

"Oh, hell," Cal said, watching it all unfold before him.

Ben choked, all effort focused on one desperate plea. "Little… help… here?"

CHAPTER NINETEEN

Ben crashed into the dresser on the far side of his bedroom. Pain shot through his right arm and coursed down his back. His body slid to the floor, the furniture slamming on its side behind him. It was one of the few pieces that reminded him of his mother, the dresser left to him after her passing. He definitely didn't have the budget for another at the moment. Not that more moments were guaranteed.

A wave of mist hovered over his bed. There should have been something to catch sight of, something tangible with a form and face to it, but after a day with Cal by his side Ben was starting to doubt his sanity on the subject. The formless fog drifting in the frozen air of the room moved in rhythm with the temperature changes, ebbing and flowing throughout the room in the blink of an eye. Like a whisper on the wind, the jet stream rushed to the corners of the room. Ben's curtains were torn from their rods and launched toward him. The cloth snapped around his wrists and pulled him into the air.

Something screamed through the mist. Cold breath wafted into Ben's face. Then he was soaring again, this time back to his bed. He bounced off the mattress, slamming face first into the nightstand. His lamp shattered under the weight, sending scraps of porcelain scattering about the growing maelstrom.

Ben was little more than a ragdoll being flipped around out of some sadistic amusement. This wasn't being committed with the same anger that came after Abigail Winslow, or Hunt, or whatever she called herself in the end. Her death had come swift and merciless. The deed had left her without a scratch in its precision. The assault on Ben, however, was going to be a prolonged act of agony.

Wallpaper tore from the walls in long swaths and grabbed at the fallen agent like tendrils. Ben rolled toward the door, kicking at the inanimate assault. He shot to his feet, a hand at his hip to draw his Ruger; he found nothing but the drawstring of his *Spider-Man* pajama pants.

The shirtless wonder threw a shrug to the silent observer at the door. It was momentary relief before the area rug beneath his bed snagged his legs, tripping him and then pulling him deeper into the room. Cold spikes scraped his skin. They ran like fingernails down his bare back. His painful cries rang out until they were lost behind the curtains wrapped tight around his neck. His feet left solid ground, or what remained of it, and he hovered in the center of the room as the unseen mist welcomed him with a wail of pleasure.

Cal remained fixed at the threshold of the room. His eyes never blinked, never strayed from the objects given life to strangle his host. Terror sat in his sky-blue orbs, a level of dread unnoticed by Ben during their time together. Ben slapped at the air, his hands unable to find a grip.

Struggling to breathe under the constricting curtains, Ben shouted, "Shoot it!"

Cal peered around the room for something, anything, to use against the invisible menace. Almost as if he were weightless, Ben flew into the back of the room. The wallpaper collected around him, locking him in place.

"Shoot it!"

Cal's eyes flared, his hands open and empty. "I'm a lawyer, remember?"

Ben spat blood on the bedroom carpet, wondering if the DSA would cover the cost for the renovation or if it would come out of his salary. He wiped his chin as he fought to regain his feet. "Not helpful, Cal!"

"I..." Cal hesitated, looking around the room quickly. He raised a finger. "I need a minute."

"What?" Ben screeched before the cord to the broken lamp snaked around his neck. Cal left the room in a hurry. *A minute. He only needs a minute.* Ben wasn't sure he had one. The invisible threat laying waste to him was no longer in a toying mood. The cord found his windpipe and cut off his airflow with a tight squeeze. Ben's back pushed against the ruined wallpaper for some leverage. It made no difference. The air in his lungs burned for release, begged for a breath not forthcoming. Ben's eyes bulged, and his cheeks flushed from the strain.

From the corner of Ben's blurred vision he caught sight of Cal returning to the room. *Any time now…* his eyes screamed to the panicked lawyer.

Cal nodded. He carried a thick black pen. He uncorked the unconventional weapon and closed the door behind him. He began to draw on the wall. Quick lines, circular in shape, started the image but it soon came into focus though Ben's own vision darkened in the corners.

His time was up. His legs no longer flailed for solid ground and his back slumped to the wall, which enveloped him eagerly. All he could hear was the thumping of his heart in his ears.

And Cal.

"Spiritus dimittere eum. Hoc in loco tutus terræ. Abscede hinc."

What his colleague said, Ben failed to understand or even recognize. The image on the wall was complete, an ornate sigil that looked similar in nature to the one found outside the comic shop that morning. Before the darkness took over Ben's vision, Cal stabbed the pen into his palm. Blood ran in small drops down his arm, and the forceful attorney slapped his bleeding hand against the marking on the wall.

"Spiritus dimittere eum. Hoc in loco tutus terræ. Abscede hinc!"

Light erupted from the mark, forcing Ben to the ground. Wallpaper surrounded him, the cord completely lifeless before him. His lungs burned as air returned in buckets to his deprived body. The agent of the DSA held tight to the floor of his bedroom, fighting to stay conscious. The chill in the air disappeared and with it any further threat.

He hoped.

Cal ran over and pried off the wallpaper covering Ben before helping him to the bed. The disoriented agent sat, and he felt his natural color slowly return to his face and hands.

"Not… bad," Ben managed to say before the pain from the effort of speaking set in. His hand cradled his neck and he touched at the indent left by the lamp cord seared to his flesh.

Cal twirled the pen between his fingers before dropping it into his waiting pocket. "You should see me with a set of watercolors." Ben tried to laugh. It hurt. Cal waved him off, noting his strain. "It won't hold forever. All I did was buy us time."

Ben closed his eyes. He imagined all the pain washing away. He didn't have time to recuperate. He needed to move. Now. His feet threatened to give out. Cal supported him, throwing him an unsure look. Ben shook his head and pointed to the mark. "How?"

"Protection sigil with a side of Latin."

Ben nodded. He kept his voice to a whisper to minimize the agony. "Something you picked up from your advocate friend?"

"I'll be sure to thank him when I get home."

"Optimistic, considering what just happened," Ben said. "What *did* just happen?"

"Do I really need to say it?"

"Okay, then, any idea what that was?" he asked, his voice hoarse. "And don't say something more ominous than a specter."

"I won't," Cal replied. His eyes no longer showed the fear they had held at the sight of the creature moments earlier. They were harder now. "I know exactly what that was. Or rather *who* that was. You just said hello to Steven Daniels."

CHAPTER TWENTY

"That was Steven Daniels?"

The question hung in the air, neither party willing to jump immediately into the conversation. Ben paced carefully between the tipped-over dresser and the peeled wallpaper scattered around the bedroom. When he reached the door, he ran his fingers over the artistic effort made on his behalf by his guest. Finally able to get a closer look at the work of art, he noticed the intricate design behind the hurried and crude scribbling. Cal had called it a shield knot. Somehow it provided supernatural protection, though how, Ben had no clue.

Ben held tight to the wall and surveyed the wreckage of the room. Had that actually happened? A ghost had attacked him? He had certainly failed to see his foe, and been unable to seize any form of footing against the opponent whipping him through the room like a ragdoll. Did that truly mean it had been a ghost though? How else could he explain it, and why did he still feel the *need* to after the evidence provided by Cal?

His father's words haunted him. His lectures about standing tall, about facing his childhood terrors and removing imagination from the equation, failed to assuage the growing doubt in his mind. The DSA didn't help either. For the last two months Ben had witnessed oddities beyond the norm—without question and without hesitation. He had powered through those doubts and done the job expected of him.

But here and now?

I can't, I still can't believe it.

Finding his balance, his leg stiff from his collision with the wall, Ben made his way into the living area, where he collapsed atop the lone recliner. Dried blood coated his arms, and bruises were forming along his neck. He sank deeper into the cushion.

Cal entered behind him, wiping sweat from his brow. Then he leaned along the back of the couch, eyes cold with the truth. "It was him, Ben."

Had Daniels somehow survived that night years ago? Ben ran through the gamut of possibilities. Some scenarios seemed completely impossible, yet maintained more credibility than Steven Daniels turning into a ghost for revenge. There were plenty of scientific angles to explore, from the mundane like gene manipulation to the obscene like cloning. None fully explained the events of the last hour, nor the massive question begging to be asked.

"Why?"

Going with Cal's theory, everything about the spirit world keyed in on certain attributes. Vengeance in the form of a specter was task-oriented. If the kill list was relegated to Winslow, then having completed the job it should have been over. Clearly, that was not the case.

"I could understand the revenge angle for Winslow—Hunt—being late for that meeting. That makes sense to me, motivation-wise. But why here? Why me?"

Cal's thumb dug into the couch's faded upholstery, lost in his musings. Ben snapped his fingers to shake his compatriot back to the conversation.

"I'm really hoping you've got something here, Cal. Evil spirits weren't covered in the DSA training program."

"It wasn't Daniels," Cal said. His hands pushed off the couch as he started to pace the room furiously.

"You just said it—"

"I know what I said," Cal said. He sighed, swallowing the frustration behind the words. "Sorry. I know, but listen. It was Daniels, but it wasn't."

Theories played behind his eyes. Ben waited, struggling to show patience at something he held so many misgivings about and had little understanding of. When Cal made his third pass of the room he pressed for more. "Then what was it? Or who? Split personality? That time of the afterlife?"

Cal stopped, a thin smirk on his lips. "Really?"

"Sorry." Ben took a deep breath. "Go ahead."

"Daniels was here, but he also wasn't," Cal resumed his pacing, his hands working out his theory as he spoke. "Someone was controlling him." Cal pointed to his weary eyes. "Blank stares—like he wasn't in the room. He was beating on you without need. It wasn't like with Winslow, which was precise. Revenge through and through. This, though? Steven Daniels doesn't know you. There is none of the vengeance seeking at play here. So..."

Ben nodded. "So someone sent him to me. How?"

Cal's eyes lit up. "Your business card. It left an imprint of your spirit or essence—whatever you want to call it. He could have tracked you down like a bloodhound. Metaphorically speaking, of course."

"I figured," Ben replied. He rubbed the bruises accumulating on his neck. Cal's shoulders slumped, and his brow creased over sullen eyes. "What's wrong? If we know someone sent him after me, then we know they did the same to Winslow. Someone we spoke with."

"Exactly," Cal shot back. He circled the couch and fell on the cushion with a loud sigh. He leaned forward, his fingers interlaced in front of him. "It's just... it's silly I guess. Pissing off the living may be fair game in this day and age, but messing with the dead like this? Controlling someone's spirit for the purpose of murder? Who would do that to someone?"

Ben forgot for a moment who was working with him. Cal, even with the loss of his family and the questions their deaths brought up every day of his life, remained innocent. He exemplified the light Ben always sought in his work. Unfortunately, the hesitant DSA agent worked with the world as it was; there were shadows even on the brightest of days.

Ben shifted to the edge of the chair. "What I need to know is how."

"A personal item and a strong connection to the deceased. And a hell of a lot of anger." Cal rubbed his temples. "Sound like anyone we spoke to yesterday?"

Out of everyone they had questioned there was only one person with that level of connection to the spirit committing murder on command. One person with the anger seeping into their words, someone who had been afraid to call Winslow by name during their meeting. And both men knew what personal item was doing the controlling. Ben stood and started for the door, the stiffness buried under a desire to close the case. "Grab your coat."

"Um, Ben?" Cal called from the couch.

Ben stopped, impatiently waiting for the hesitant attorney. Cal pointed at the man to showcase his outfit. Ben peered down at his naked chest and the pajama bottom ensemble, suddenly much colder for the realization.

"Spider-Man PJs might not be the best approach," Cal joked.

"Right," Ben muttered. He closed the apartment door. As he headed for the bedroom he grabbed Cal's coat and tossed it to him. "I'll get dressed," Ben said, on the move. "*Then* we go catch a killer."

CHAPTER TWENTY-ONE

For a very long, chilled second Morgan thought her life was over. Lincoln's cold eyes stared down the barrel of his .357 Magnum, the laser sight aimed at her chest. In that instant she believed she had underestimated the situation; she had underestimated how far her colleague had fallen. It had been days since his last attempt to reach out to her. His call for help had gone unanswered by the occupied agent of the DSA. For all these reasons and more she thought she would die in an auto yard outside Silver Spring. Alone.

Then Lincoln grinned.

Breath returned to her lungs, and the cold gusts worked to freeze her insides. Little snowflakes filled the air around them. The weather turned bitter and snow piled at their feet.

The man she had come to find, to help, holstered his sidearm. "Had to be sure you came alone," he said without looking. "Precaution."

"Of course," Morgan said, drawing out the words. He kept his distance near an old Chevy Celebrity wagon, its windows shattered and frame semi-crushed. "What is this all about, Lincoln? What if I *had* come with backup? Hell, even just Riley?"

"I get it, Morgan." His look softened and she fell back on her heels, relaxing slightly. "I honestly don't know how it would have played."

Comfort left quickly, and her arms crossed against her chest. "Not what I want to hear. You've got a lot of folks worried about you. I'm starting to think maybe with good reason."

"Hey," barked Lincoln. His eyes went cold, white orbs mixing with the increasing snowfall surrounding them. "I reached out to you. *I did that.*"

"And I came," she replied. "So tell me what happened."

"I..." He turned away, eyes lowering. "I don't know."

"Come on, Lincoln."

"Morgan..."

She couldn't believe his hesitation. Frustration snapped in her. *So much for keeping things civil,* she thought, her face flush with anger. "Two men are dead, Lincoln! Did they trip and shoot themselves? Quite the feat."

"They weren't supposed to be there." His arms spread wide. "Hell, no one should have been. But he knew, Morgan. He knew about my past at the Savery. And those two? They were after him."

"The Witness?"

He nodded. "He knew. Everything."

"He was waiting for you?" she asked, confused. "To what? Have a chat? Did he need a fourth player for bridge?"

Lincoln threw her a hard glare. "He said he had answers. That we're being played. He told me the DSA isn't what it seems."

That was what it always came back to—the DSA. The secrets kept behind Metcalf's locked door—the secrets held above them all. Morgan recalled the exhaustion tucked under the director's swollen lids, the growing concern over Lincoln's actions in Des Moines.

Then there was Riley's absence from not only the mission but the office in general. Morgan had come to know him, at least on some surface level, over their time together. His absence meant more than what Metcalf alluded to that morning. All workplaces held something back from their employees. The DSA was no different.

Whatever mistrust she held with Metcalf never reflected the work being done, work Morgan fully believed in. To imagine nefarious dealings occurring under the surface, that they were being used for someone else's agenda instead of the greater good for the country, was not even a possibility for her. Not to mention the fact the information had come from a man who had murdered seven thousand people in Bellbrook.

Lincoln believed, though, and that worried her. The startled awe when he referred to the Witness knowing more than he should.

"You can't be serious, Lincoln." Her eyes fell on her holster. Still unclipped. "You believed him?"

"He showed me who killed Morrison Engers. The man I was supposed to protect. The man I..." Lincoln fell silent and raised a hand to his bloodshot eyes. "I don't know what to think anymore."

Morgan pressed, "It sure as hell sounds like you do."

"I said I don't."

"He killed an entire town!" Morgan said, moving forward. She reached out to Lincoln and he pulled back and shook his head. One second he appeared full of bile, yet lost and confused the next.

"He says he was protecting them."

"Convenient," she scoffed. The cold ripped through her just as easily as Lincoln's defense of the man who took Ruth Heller from them. Ruth and so many more. "Also, complete and utter nonsense. What were you doing in that room, Lincoln?"

"Metcalf sent me to find him."

"She told me."

"Everything?" Lincoln said. "She wanted him dead. No questions asked. Don't you find that strange?"

A sanctioned killing by the Director of the DSA? *Strange* barely started to cover it. No matter the number of deaths tallied in Bellbrook, Morgan refused to let go of due process. What the hell had Metcalf been thinking? What was Lincoln?

"You accepted," she said, disappointed. Her gaze thinned. "Is he dead?"

"No." Lincoln removed his hat, his hand running through his tightly trimmed hair. Wet beads of melting snow mixed with sweat fell to the cold concrete beneath them. "I wanted to do it, Morgan. For Ruth. For everything he did in Bellbrook. But he knew things. Answers to what we're working against."

Purpose. It had always been important to Lincoln. He mentioned as much in the hospital after their mission in Bellbrook while recuperating from a gunshot to his right arm. He had begged her for an answer about what was happening out in the world, about what they were fighting against and for whom, but she'd had no response. No answer at all.

"Then the others showed up," he continued, shaking her

from memory. "They were going to finish the job for me, but I... I couldn't let them."

Her eyes widened at the confession. "You killed two people, Lincoln. They were military men who served this country. And you killed them to protect the Witness?"

He shook his head furiously. She could tell there was more to it—more to his time in Des Moines. His inability to look her in the eyes confirmed more hid beneath the surface. More than he could put into words. He offered her nothing in terms of a defense for the loss of life. No regret. No apology. Two were dead. That was the only truth, no matter the reasons behind the story. Two were dead, and the mass murderer in the room had gotten a pass.

"I couldn't..." Lincoln's nostrils flared in frustration. His hand slammed against his leg while he fought for the right words. "Morgan, listen to me. Just listen. What if he's right?"

"What?" Her blood went cold at the question.

His eyes pleaded. "What if he's telling the truth?"

"About what?" Morgan yelled, her words echoing in the center of the kill box.

"Anything! Everything!" His arms reached for her and found only emptiness. Her fingers inched closer to her Glock. "Morgan. What if there's a chance he can do more, that he can save us from what's coming—"

"Which is what, Lincoln? Did he drop that little nugget? Or was he too busy turning you against the DSA? Against your friends? Against *me*?"

A deep breath escaped his lungs, the mist rising above them into the night sky before fading from view. "He disappeared before I could ask."

Morgan shook her head. "Like I said before. Convenient."

This was why Metcalf sent her. Out of everyone, every agent at Metcalf's disposal, it had to be her. Not for the secrecy of the mission, though that played a role for the director. No, it was for this moment—the moment where Lincoln's story fell apart. Where his pleading eyes begged for help and where anyone else may have fallen for them—given him the benefit of the doubt for the time he served the agency. Morgan couldn't. She'd been in Bellbrook. She had been in a *dozen* Bellbrooks since her time in the DSA and before as a medic. She had witnessed death and destruction up close and no reason ever justified it.

Lincoln tried all the same. "Morgan. Something is wrong with the DSA. The things we've seen. Grissom. Ruth. It isn't natural. Someone is manipulating the field. Playing a game with our lives, and the Witness knows about it. You have to see that."

She nodded slowly. Her hand no longer hid its intentions as she released the Glock from her hip holster. "I do. I see it, Lincoln."

"Morgan," he begged, his body backing up against the Chevy Celebrity as white as the snow coating the ground between them.

"I wish there was another way, Lincoln," Morgan explained. The gun sat heavy in her hands; her chest felt heavier from the weight of her actions. "Right now, though? I need to see your hands."

CHAPTER TWENTY-TWO

"Got the message again? Good luck with that."

The sardonic charm of Ben's voice chirped in the ear of Director Susan Metcalf. It was her tenth unsuccessful attempt to connect with the man not seen since leaving Fort Meade with the Grissom File. One message for every hour since a report had found its way to her desk detailing the death of Agent Abigail Winslow in a location that surprised her: down the hall from her selected apartment for Ben. The voicemail prompt had lost its whimsical appeal after the first call. The rapidity of its access told her she was being ignored. Ben did not want to talk.

Too bad, she thought, slamming the phone down on the desk. She needed him on board. She needed to explain things, finally. There were secrets to be shared and shuffled aside. Work to be done. She snatched the phone from the desk and redialed his cell. Only a single ring chimed in her ear before the message began again.

"Son of a bitch," she muttered. The phone was silenced, the screen falling face down on her mess of a desk. Though she had been in the office for over sixteen hours, little in the way of actual work had been completed. There were the usual updates from department heads to be approved. She ignored them. Transfers and after-action reports waited for review. *They could wait indefinitely*, she lied to herself.

The fact remained, things had spiraled away from her. Missed opportunities equaled mistakes, the very thing she couldn't afford with Sullivan down the hall. Though she had failed to notice it at first, the deputy director had been on site more often since the Bellbrook affair. His mark had been placed on everything. The latest included the hiring of the now-deceased Agent Winslow, the beginning and end of her relationship with Metcalf steeped in mystery.

She hated the feeling. Questions had been left unresolved with Winslow's death. Sullivan had planted her in the department. He had approved her placement in the same building as Ben, the very same agent Sullivan had held an impromptu hearing with, in an effort to compromise his position. All without her knowing.

The Council had cut her out of the loop, feeding the day-to-day agenda to her subordinate, who had then kept vital information from her. It was intolerable and had to change. The 'how' of it escaped her at the moment. The why of it did as well. Sullivan had played her. He fed her a line of bull with every exchange, leading her to an endgame she had failed to envision.

She needed Ben on her side. Her field team was all she had, yet it had shattered like glass before her. Ben avoided her. Lincoln held two counts of murder against him. Metcalf hoped Morgan would be able to speak with him, get him to see the light, but even her stalwart agent held misgivings about Metcalf's command of the team in light of her recent missteps, all stemming from the loss of Jacob Grissom.

She needed all the help she could get, but it was rapidly dissolving. The research team sat secure in Sullivan's pocket. *His* kind face greeted them, not hers. She had made it her mission to keep the trains running, to not be a friend—another mistake. Sullivan had seized upon her error as his time in the warehouse increased. Why hadn't she seen it coming?

Even Zac. Tracking personnel was never something she had wanted to do. Monitoring their terminals, following the flow of information, including all requests made, was not something necessary at one time. Ben's assessment had cemented her current outlook. Seeing the logs of inquiries made on her personal files by Zac shocked the director. Things were bad between them, the lack of trust her own doing from the work over the last few months. To see him in Sullivan's pocket, tracking her and monitoring privileged information, gnawed at her.

Who was there left for her to trust?

In answer, the door opened. It startled the overtired woman in the pleated skirt, causing her hands to tighten their grip on the arms of the leather chair. In the dim light of the office, Stephanie Atwater stepped inside.

"Director?"

"Stephanie?" Metcalf waved her in. "I didn't realize you were here. What time…?" The pile of unread reports buried her desk clock. She shifted them aside with a small thud. It was almost one in the morning. *Where did the evening go?* Stephanie threw her a look of concern. "You should be home. Bed. Boyfriend. A life."

Stephanie smiled, closing the door. "Oh to dream. I work when you work, Director. Rules are rules."

Metcalf shook her head. That had never been a rule, not one she would have forced on anyone. Still, she appreciated the thought. "Thank you."

"Can I bring you something?"

Metcalf pulled her hair back and straightened herself in her chair. She paused a long moment before offering the chair across the desk. "A friendly ear?"

Stephanie's smile faded. "That bad?"

Metcalf smirked, a huff of breath escaping her. She reached into her desk drawer and removed a small box no larger than a lighter. On top was a small switch, which she clicked on, allowing the node to beam red at its activation.

"What is — ?"

Metcalf held up a lone finger, interrupting the question. The red light of the switch intensified and showered over the room. At the end of the sweep, the device faded to black.

"Surveillance tech," Metcalf said. "Sweeps the room every minute and neutralizes any listening devices within range."

She had found the first bug upon returning from Fort Meade; it was an obvious plant under her desk, one she should have expected after their confrontation. She had cursed her lack of preparation on that front, believing her position to be impervious to scrutiny — at least from those under her purview.

She had been wrong and immediately started using the device. There would be no more leaked information or looking over her shoulder — at least from the confines of her office. It was safe. Possibly the last safe place left in Metcalf's world.

"Forget my last comment," Stephanie said, eyes aglow at the call for such equipment. "This is a whole new level of bad."

Stephanie sat, then leaned close to the desk. Metcalf saw much of herself in the young woman she had brought on as her assistant—driven and passionate about life. At least, that's how Metcalf thought she once was. Now, there was nothing but closed doors and distance from everyone and everything. More mistakes.

"It's time, Steph," Metcalf said. The forty-year-old woman stood, her hands kneading the gold chain around her neck. Reaching into her blouse she retrieved the key that hung from the chain.

"Susan." Stephanie's voice was low. "I realize there are things going on I'm not cleared for, but to go that far…"

Metcalf stopped. "You know me better than to exaggerate." The director's gaze fell on the wall. Above the credenza in the corner of the room, which was stocked with a pitcher of water and personal coffee machine, was a single painting. It showed a yellow farmhouse surrounded by a white picket fence. It always caused her lips to curl. Metcalf slowly removed it from the hook on the wall to reveal a small wall safe. "The truth is, I have an agent wanted for murder, another unreachable and most likely compromised, one dead, and the last? Well, something is going on with Morgan."

Metcalf's sigh was muffled by the sound of the key slipping into the lock. The door opened with a loud thunk. Her fingers deftly fell on a single slip of paper, then removed it from the confines of the safe. Her heels clicked loudly along the tile back to her chair.

"Listen to me complain," she said. She sank into the chair and rubbed her brow. "When did it get so complicated?"

Stephanie looked toward the door. "It's the deputy director, isn't it?"

"And more," Metcalf replied. She held out the paper. The slight hands of the young woman across from her accepted it. "It's time."

"Are you sure?" she said, scanning the list. "We've talked about this before, but I never thought, never actually considered you going through with this."

"No choice." Metcalf mirrored her misgivings. The list meant walking away from the DSA, from the work she had committed to a decade earlier. It meant trusting outsiders and risking everything. But it was fast becoming necessary, thanks to Sullivan. "Bunker Protocol, Stephanie. Let our people know."

Stephanie held her tongue for a long moment. Questions writhed to escape her thin lips, but the young assistant was better than that. She knew once the protocol went live, things would move quickly.

"I'll make the arrangements."

Metcalf stopped her at the door. "Tell no one."

Her confidant turned with a smile. "Rules are rules."

The door closed with the soft clasp of metal in the frame. Solitude returned to the office. Metcalf's shoulders slumped. Rules *were* rules. She lived by them in the past. They molded her life, her decisions, and the paths taken to achieve what she had at such a young age. This was different, however. To protect the DSA, to have any hope of saving what came next, it was time to break expectations.

And long past time to change the rules.

CHAPTER TWENTY-THREE

Ben's hand stayed close to his holster and the Ruger within. His fingers were freezing from the wintry air of the pre-dawn hours over Bethesda. His steps shuffled along the concrete pavers, and his body struggled to move forward without pausing between each footfall. Cal kept close behind, hands buried deep into the pockets of his overcoat.

Both were exhausted. The few hours of sleep accumulated before Stephen Daniels' extremely rude wakeup call had done little to rejuvenate the pair from their endless hunt for Abigail Winslow's killer. Sleep sounded like heaven, but it would not come, not until the threat was eliminated.

Daniels' interruption came with good news, however. It had given them a name, the answer to their interviews from the previous day.

It had given them Megan Daniels.

The Cape Cod on Westlake no longer sparkled from the brightly painted shutters along the white siding. With the shadow of night still upon the yard, the Daniels' home was dark and foreboding. The clouds above seemed too low to be natural. They shifted fast overhead, swirling around with the blowing wind.

Ben cleared his throat. "I'll do the talking."

"Good." Cal nodded. He stared ahead at the darkness surrounding the home.

"No argument?" Ben shot his partner a curious glance. "I was really hoping for an argument."

"Do you *want* me to do the talking?"

For as much as the home looked less than inviting to Ben, it was what waited within that caused him to hesitate at the base of the front porch. He felt the bruising along his neck and the split skin running up his arms. He wanted to turn around, wanted to call it in and let someone else handle it. There were others far more qualified for the work.

Cal had mentioned it previously, though he knew experts on ghosts were few and far between. Still, Ben remained locked on the front door. The white sheen, once appearing immaculate during their previous visit, looked cracked and peeling.

The Ruger slipped into his waiting hand. Ben turned to Cal, shaking his head. "No."

"Cause I can," Cal said. "Probably better coming from me anyway." Ben cocked an eyebrow at the brazen confidence of his colleague. The young attorney only shrugged. "No gun."

Ben gripped his sidearm tighter at its mention. Taking the steps in one solid jump, he moved for the door. He knocked loudly on the frame, then peered back to Cal, who remained along the stone walkway with eyes wandering back to the rental car on the street.

"You shouldn't even be here," Ben said.

"I can stay in the car."

"Cal." Ben hoped his fear was well hidden. When he closed his eyes, even in a momentary blink, he was a boy again wishing his father would take away the nightmares. There would always be fear, fear of the unknown, fear that making a mistake meant a loss of life, fear he wouldn't stack up against the growing obstacles in his path.

Cal nodded, reading Ben's hesitation. He stepped up to the porch. "I'm right behind you."

The comfort behind the thought faded with the creaking of footsteps behind the door. "Great. Here we go."

The door opened with a crash, causing Ben and Cal to step back. Cal's hand gripped the railing of the porch. His heels threatened to topple off the edge.

Megan stood in the doorway, a pale nightgown clinging to the curves of her body. Glassy and distant eyes met them. Her long fingers played with the chain around her neck. The door slipped from her hand, and she moved deeper into the darkness of the home, beckoning them inside.

"Agent," she said with a whisper. "Mr. Cooper."

Ben shared a glance with his hesitant colleague before following her. Cal shook his head, ushering the armed agent forward. They stepped into the small foyer and the front door slammed into its frame. Megan leaned against the banister of the stairwell.

"You don't seem surprised to see us, Mrs. Daniels," Ben said, scanning the lower level of the home. No misty breath. No visible residue of Megan's secret weapon anywhere in sight. None of the signs Cal had mentioned over the course of their time together.

"Should I be?" she asked with a smile, apparently noticing his concern. Under the warm lights of the sun the previous day her smile had appeared genuine, almost glowing. Now her skin was pale and her lips were tinted blood red. "Would you prefer it if I played the victim more, Agent Riley?"

Damn right I would, he thought, stepping deeper into the foyer. "What really happened to your husband, Megan?"

Her hand grazed the necklace at the mention of the deceased. Her eyes thinned. "He died. Like I told you."

"There was more to it, though, wasn't there?" Ben pressed. "Abigail Hunt wasn't at the meeting for a reason. It was more than a simple traffic jam."

"She killed him."

"How?"

"She offered him up!" Megan spat at them. "She ratted him out to keep her cover. She murdered my husband."

They should have suspected more when they interviewed her. The home was a shrine to the past left in the wake of her husband's murder. She had been unable to move forward with her life after his death. She held the same job, stayed in the same home with the same shared possessions, as if he were still around. Then there was the way she spoke about Winslow. Megan never mentioned her husband's partner by name. Even now, she couldn't say the name of the woman she hated more than anyone in the world.

Ben threw Cal a quick glance. The young lawyer from Albany shook his head and continued to search the area. Ben had to rely on his colleague for his second sight; he was grateful Cal willfully put his life into the thick of things, though he was also wary of the selflessness. Enough blood had been spilled during their investigation. He didn't want to see anything happen to the man he was quickly calling friend.

"You killed her for revenge," Ben continued, turning back to the grinning woman at the base of the stairs.

"They told me what happened—Steven's friends. What she did to him. I was so angry, but she was gone. Like a ghost." More laughter, deeper now, bubbled out of her. "And then I saw her. At the market, of all places. The one we always went to. Like nothing happened. She was just living her life while he was dead."

It would have been easy to follow the unsuspecting Abigail Hunt, now Abigail Winslow, from the market to her new apartment. Cal accomplished that much, driven by his own obsession with the deceased woman.

Ben shook his head. "You didn't have to kill her."

"I did what any loving wife would do for her husband," she snapped.

"You're not doing this for Steven," Cal replied, catching her anger with his soulful eyes. She needed to hear him directly, needed to be willing to hear anything other than the sound of her own regret and her desire for revenge.

"I do *everything* for him," her voice boomed along the stairwell. "Everything."

"You think so," Cal persisted. "But you're killing him over and over again by not moving on."

Air whirled around the second-floor landing in a wave. Both men let the breath out of their lungs at the same moment as they watched it escape in a shallow mist and rise above them. It was getting noticeably colder in the room.

"Move on to what?" Megan shouted, the air above gathering mass swirling faster and faster. "He was my life! We were supposed to start a family! She took my life, so I took hers!"

Ben raised his sidearm. He gripped it with both hands, and leveled it on the raging woman. "Don't do anything rash, Megan."

"Rash?" Megan scoffed. "Is that what you call protecting your family?"

"Ben?" Cal called, though his voice was only a distant whisper.

Ben remained fixed on the swirling air. Growing, swelling, it took shape over the crazed widow. "Please, Megan. Please calm down. I'm sorry for what happened to Steven. I am. But this accomplishes nothing."

"That's where you're wrong, Agent Riley."

"Ben?" Cal's voice pleaded, his feet falling back toward the front door. There was fear in Cal's eyes, the same fear Ben had attempted to tuck away ever since he heard the word ghost enter the equation. The swirling air above them gained the shape of what was once a man. "Ben, I think we should —"

"No one is going to break up our love again," Megan said with a cackle, crazed eyes bearing down on them. "Ever."

A face broke through the mist, gnarled features bent and torn from the veil. The decayed essence of Stephen Daniels, a man who had served his country proudly and died for it, screamed in the darkness of the Cape Cod. With blistering eyes of white, the specter greeted his prey. For the first time, Ben caught sight of the being.

"Is that…?"

Cal nodded from the periphery. Steven rushed toward them, screaming like the wind. Megan smiled wide and pointed to them.

"Show our guests out, would you, dear?"

CHAPTER TWENTY-FOUR

His expectations, those played to and those ingrained, had remained despite the mounting evidence to the contrary. For Ben, they were still those of an eight-year-old kid, nestled under the covers while listening to his father's strong-willed words about the world. The nightmares lingered only in his mind, a fantasy of imagination and fear overcoming the reality surrounding them in the small nook of a bedroom. Monsters were imaginary, able to be overcome and discarded.

The hope remained, even with Cal's explanation of Winslow's death. Throughout their investigation Cal had pushed for a singular threat, one never seen by Ben. Even in his struggle against the shapeless void in his bedroom earlier that evening, he continued to doubt their suspect despite the mounting evidence.

Ghosts weren't real. They couldn't exist—much less kill—not without some sign, some knowledge by people. In a world where every damn slip of the tongue was monitored and shared on fifteen different forums within seconds of escaping into the air, how could no one have learned the truth about the spirit world?

"Holy shit," Ben uttered, mouth agape at the floating figure rushing toward them. "Ghosts are real."

Stark realization gripped the frozen agent. Where once he'd imagined learning a true flesh-and-blood killer was responsible for the murder of a colleague, now no doubt existed to the truth of the matter. Beyond that, however, was the fact that Cal's gifts were real. The rules were real, and the spirit world was as dark and ugly as their own. Ben witnessed it as clear as the man at his side.

No nightmares came close to the terror spreading throughout his body.

"Why can I see him now?" Ben asked. The question wasn't meant to be his top priority. Moving out of the grim specter's path was more pressing, yet he had to know.

"Because of her," Cal said, pointing to the joyful figure at the foot of the stairs. "Our proximity to Megan is bringing Steven out, connecting us to him just as strongly as he is to her."

"Right." Ben raised his sidearm at the pale woman. Megan's hand grazed the charm at her neck. "Stop this, Megan! Stop it now!"

Her laughter boomed. "And if I say no?"

A candlestick sconce ripped from the closest wall and shot across the room. It whacked Ben's wrist. His Ruger clattered from his grasp to the floor below. He bent to grab it, but his hand swiped air instead.

"What the—?" He was floating, lifted from the ground. Steven Daniels forced him away from the fallen weapon. Ben struggled to reconnect with the hardwood floor of the foyer. The specter grinned maliciously and waved his hand to the left. "Oh, hell."

Ben flew, his body out of his control. He blasted into the living room, slamming against the couch, then bounced into the mantel. His head cracked against the brickwork and he collapsed to the ground.

The world spun. The shadows of the living room blurred around Ben. He struggled to his knees, and his hand instinctively went to the back of his head. Blood ran from his fingers.

"Let's not do that again," he muttered. He was grateful his skull was intact after the collision. The specter was before him as he stood. Tendril fingers reached for Ben. The agent cocked his fist and barreled forward with a haymaker. It sailed through the mist, and the bewildered Ben staggered with the blow. He stared at his fist. "Well, that just isn't fair."

A blanket was ripped from the back of the couch and flew through the air like a kite lost in a storm. The fleece material snaked around Ben's arms and torso, tying tight in the back. Feet no longer rested on the ground and he was hurled to the mantel once more, pinned by the force of Steven's anger.

A gift offered for his wife.

"Cal!" Ben exclaimed. The edges of the blanket looped, jamming into his gaping mouth to quiet his call for help.

The attorney was already moving, though the act was too late. The Ruger was out of reach. Megan's pale fingers cradled the delicate weapon. She lifted the strange instrument with wild eyes, burning with excitement at its potential.

Cal reeled back on his feet, a hand raised in defense. She cocked the hammer and aimed the gun at the living room and the rest of their party.

"You talk of fairness, Agent Riley?" Megan said. "That woman earned what happened to her. Her death was the very definition of fair. She took my husband from me. We were happy, and she ruined it. I won't let you take him from me too."

"Don't do this, Megan," Cal begged. Ben's eyes grew wide, part of him pleading for assistance while the larger part hoped to save the innocent man from danger. The blanket tightened with each moan from the hovering specter before him.

"You never should have come here," Megan said. She extended the gun, both hands on the grip to steady her aim.

"No!" Cal leapt at her, knocking the gun down and away just as the chamber emptied with a boom. It echoed in the room, the bullet smashing inches from Ben's leg, shattering a pair of images hanging along the wall. The photos of a couple fully in love broke upon the ground.

Cal struggled for the weapon, Megan clawing back at her attacker. The specter hesitated during their melee. The break allowed breath to return to Ben as he coughed the blanket loose from his lips. Steven's spirit stared, conflicted by the pair of intruders and unsure where to strike.

"Let go!" she screeched, knocking him aside. The gun remained hers, and her fingers stayed locked along the trigger.

Cal rolled from the blow, then jumped to his feet. His right hand clenched tight at his side, while his left reached out for the woman. "Can't you see the pain you're causing him? Look at him. He isn't at peace. This isn't right. You *know* that, Megan. You do."

"No." The widow resisted, and she rose up to face him. She wiped her hair from her face Her grin grew in the shadows of the home. "We belong together. Forever! Right, baby?"

The specter turned to Ben, teeth like razors in his misty mouth. The floating figure waved his hand to the right and Ben left the comfort of the mantel. His body, weightless once more, careened off the standing lamp in the corner of the room and bounced against the window frame at the front of the domicile before finally hitting the ground.

"Please," he whispered, though the word was cut off by the tightening coils of the blanket. More blankets shot from around the room, binding his legs and trapping him in place. His lungs burned, oxygen forced out by the ghost's actions.

"Call him off," Cal announced, strength behind the words.

Megan turned the gun on him. "Or what?"

"Or say goodbye." Cal opened his clenched fist. Sitting along his palm rested a pink butterfly charm on a gold chain.

Megan snatched at her neck, but the keepsake was no longer present. Fear took hold, her one source of comfort stolen from her. The specter's anger diminished, and the brief pause allowed Ben deep gulps of air.

"Do it, Cal!" he cried from the floor. "Do it now!"

The specter woke from the distraction, smothering Ben's mouth and nose with more furnishings from the room. The ensnared agent's lungs cried for release as the pressure tightened.

Hurry, Cal…

CHAPTER TWENTY-FIVE

Plaster tore from the walls. A bullet whizzed in front of the fleeing Cal as he turned the corner from the living room back into the foyer. The house ran in a loop offering little in the way of cover. Outside was no help, and time was not on his side. Nothing really was at the moment.

Upstairs it is.

Cal bounded up the steps, another shot missing his ankle at the last moment. The charm warmed his palm. He took the steps two at a time, whipping around on the second-floor landing as Megan began her pursuit.

Ducking into the farthest room from the stairs, Cal pushed the door tight to the frame without closing it completely. His heart pounded in his ears. This was never what he wanted, never what he had imagined when he woke in the hospital after his car accident. His life until then had been normal, almost predictable for a well-to-do bookworm with dreams of following his father's footsteps in the courtroom. He hadn't wanted to do it out of a sense of entitlement or even for the hope of a proud smile from the old man, but a genuine desire to help those in need.

He'd hoped to face the challenges that came with the law to make a difference for those unable to fight back. Violence had never played into it. Conflict of a physical nature had been anathema to Cal. In his mind, words had always won the day.

He opened his fist, the charm glittering in the dim light of the moon. Words were all the weapon he ever needed. *Well, that and a little luck.*

"He's my husband!" Megan bellowed from the landing. Her

steps were soft as she crept closer. Cal left the comfort of the door, and grabbed the garbage can in the corner. He skirted around the bed for the far side of the room. Megan's words obscured his movements. "My one love! You can't take him from me!"

The floor creaked across the hall. The door slammed open and banged against the wall, the sudden shift causing Cal to gasp and drop the ring. It fell into the garbage, coming to rest at the bottom of the metal tin with tissues and little else. Cal reached for the inside breast pocket of his coat and the one item he had hoped to avoid using. Unfortunately, it was now absolutely required to save Ben's life and end this nightmare once and for all.

He opened the small canister of lighter fluid and poured the contents into the wastebasket on top of the charm. A match broke loose from the pack, though he hesitated to strike.

Behind him, the door opened. Megan's eyes widened. In her terror, her fingers slammed against the trigger of the gun. A pair of shots snapped through the air. Cal dove to the ground and the match slipped from his hand. He cursed, fighting the pack to remove another.

"Steven's already gone, Megan," Cal shouted from the floor. Her steps slowed at the sound of his voice. His words were all he had left to fight for time. He hoped she might actually hear him this time. "You have to face that. Accept it. Your husband died."

"He was stolen from me," she replied. Her feet stomped along the carpet. "I won't let it happen again!"

She rounded the bed, a wicked sneer returning to her lips at the sight of Cal lying on his back with nothing more than a matchstick between his fingers. The gun, now an extension of her resolve, was aimed at his head. No hesitation remained in her eyes, no regret at the necessity of the moment. Her husband was all that mattered, despite all rational thought in the matter. She pulled the trigger.

Only to hear the click of the chamber.

Empty.

Cal struck the match against the pack, the soft flame sparking. He held it over the garbage at his side. "I'm sorry."

"No!"

He dropped it and the flames exploded in a flash of color against the shadows. Cal rolled away from the trash can, then bounced to his feet. Megan jumped for the basket and, in her haste, the gun dropped from her hands. She fought to reach the butterfly charm as the fire danced in her deep orbs. He blocked her from the act. He clutched her wrists and forced her away. He used his body to cut off her view as the keepsake, her lifeline to her husband, burned in the heat.

The plastic melted. The colors bled and obscured the image. Megan's nails dug into his skin and he cried out, releasing her. She delivered a sharp right cross that sent him reeling away.

"What have you done?"

Cal rubbed at his split lip. "What you should have done. Let him go."

Megan shook her head, then turned from the raging flames as a shrill cry rose from the living room below.

CHAPTER TWENTY-SIX

The room darkened. The constricting threads squeezed Ben from head to toe, bringing him to the brink of unconsciousness. He fought for time, battled against the inevitable even as the chasms where Steven's eyes had once been burrowed through him in anticipation.

This couldn't be the end. Not after everything, not with so many questions left unanswered. The Grissom File remained on his desk. Sullivan and Metcalf both waited for his response — for a choice to be made. The future waited for Ben to take the first step, and now he wondered if it would always remain that way: if he would float through the afterlife angry at the loss of time, at his indecision and the days swept away because of it.

No. I won't let it.

Ben stretched against the fleece tying his arms to his sides. He kicked at the knots locking his feet together. Every ounce of will flooded his being against the growing darkness enveloping him. There had to be a sign of light, a trickle of hope left. Something for Ben to grab, to snatch from the hands of a cruel fate no one deserved. Not Jacob Grissom. Not Ruth Heller. Not even Abigail Winslow and Steven Daniels.

And sure as hell not Benjamin Harrison Riley.

Unfortunately, there was no leverage to be gained. Not with the specter looming over him, maliciously sabotaging his every effort. Steven, or what remained of the once-proud federal agent, wanted Ben dead, and no amount of resistance seemed to counter that drive. With each twitch of his elongated, slender fingers, the twisted chords tightened around the dying man.

Then the ghost screamed. It was a hideous screech of pain

that echoed in the room, piercing Ben's ears. The fading agent slammed against the ground. The knots that had been securing him, squeezing every last drop of life from him, slackened. Breath returned and he clawed at his throat, coughing with each intake. Spots ran along his vision, but through them all he saw was Steven's spirit bellowing against the end.

Eyes of white blazed and sparked like candles. His tendril-like fingers snapped, adding to the howl filling the room. All control dissipated. The anger and rage shifted to terror. Ben reached for the man, but his hand fell through Steven's arm to the ground. The mist spread thinner and dissolved before his eyes.

"No..."

Megan rounded the bottom of the stairwell and faltered at the sight of her husband. Steven glowed bright, beaming beneath the veneer of darkness created by his wife. The specter pleaded. His sadness matched the tears that ran down Megan's cheeks.

There was no help, no other way for this to end. When Cal entered the room, Ben realized what had happened: the only choice available to them.

"Don't, Megan," Cal said. "Don't look at him as he is, as you made him. Remember him how he lived."

"No," she sobbed. "Don't let this happen."

"It already has," Cal replied, hand to her shoulder. "You already lost him. Now you have to let him go."

Steven screamed. The flames that had destroyed the butterfly charm began to consume his misty form.

"Baby!"

A burst of light, and then Steven was gone. The specter was no more—only a memory to be carried by a grieving widow for the rest of her days.

A hand reached for Ben and helped him to his feet. Cal offered a sad smile, the feeling shared in the moment. Both were sullen from the loss, yet grateful at what had been saved thanks to Cal's actions.

Megan collapsed in the silence of the living room. "He's gone. I lost him again."

Cal shook his head. He knelt beside her, a hand wiping at her tear. He lifted her fallen gaze from the spot where her husband had left her for the second time.

"That's one way to see it, Megan," Cal said, his words soft and slow between her sobs. "But only one. Hopefully someday you'll figure that out."

CHAPTER TWENTY-SEVEN

She didn't believe him. Lincoln inched back against the driver-side door of the Chevy Celebrity. Morgan's gun remained poised to fire, her eyes thin slits of white in the growing darkness surrounding them. The snow slowed, but the freeze continued, cutting through the hidden layers of Kevlar beneath his fleece jacket.

It was a tough sell. There was always going to be a less-than-good chance she would understand his point of view when it came to the Witness. He understood her reticence, even sided with it more often than not. But he no longer stood one hundred percent behind the DSA's policy when it came to the man who had murdered an entire town. A chance existed, even if infinitesimal, the Witness' claim of protection over the town was legitimate. His promise of answers kept Lincoln from returning to his position as a member of the Department of Special Assignments. Lincoln knew it to be true, especially since the revelation about Morrison Engers' murder had been proven thanks to his visit to Des Moines. How could he doubt the rest?

Truth be told, there was no going back for him.

"I'm sorry, Lincoln," Morgan said, fully aware of the fact neither wanted to say aloud. She took a step forward, but was careful not to extend too far, too quickly. "I need you to come in. Now."

"I get that. I do." He tried to wave her back, his eyes begging for another minute. He just needed to find the right words—to say it in the right way so that she would understand the conflict at hand.

"Men are dead." Her words felt like bullets tearing into his flesh. She held such disdain for his actions. Any justification from Lincoln appeared impossible to accept. "The Witness is in the wind and you have a connection with him. You can see the problem here, can't you?"

Lincoln hadn't thought of that. For as much as he wanted to convince Morgan of his sincerity, he had never considered the DSA's interest in his actions. Beyond the scandal they would cause, there was the Witness to consider. They wanted him just as much as Army Intelligence and who knew how many others.

"Morgan—"

She shook her head. "No, Lincoln. Not another word."

"Right." His hand slipped into the open space where the driver's-side window had once been. His fingers peeled back the tape he had placed along the inner frame of the vehicle.

His eyes remained on Morgan and her gun. "He's a murderer, Lincoln. He's not here to help anyone. There are no answers down that road."

"What if you're wrong, Morgan?" Lincoln replied. The tape pulled loose and his hand gripped tight to a peach-sized orb. He raised it out of the car. "I can't take that chance."

His thumb snatched the pin and pulled it loose from the sphere. Morgan's eyes widened and she rushed toward him. "Don't, Lincoln, just—"

"I'm sorry, Morgan." The pin fell to the ground with a soft clang. Lincoln tossed the grenade out like a tennis ball. It landed four feet in front of the ill-prepared agent.

"Linc—" Her words were lost as the darkness exploded in a field of white light. The flash grenade did its job admirably, coating the area with a close-up fireworks display.

When it faded she stood alone in the box he had created. Morgan remained dazed for a minute, disoriented from the explosion. Her movements were staggered. The aggravated agent spun in circles around the area, searching the box for some sign of life—for some sign of Lincoln.

Lincoln, however, rested comfortably in the nest he'd built earlier out of the backseat of an old Dodge Charger. It sat among the ruins scattered throughout the junkyard. From his vantage he had a clear view of the four pillars of cars making up the kill box and the lone woman at its center.

She would never find him. He had spent too much time anticipating every contingency, every possible outcome. Charges had been set along the pillars if she hadn't come alone or if others interrupted their conversation. There was also the rifle by his side—a last resort in his mind. His fingers grazed the barrel, keeping it within reach as his eyes followed Morgan throughout the junkyard.

There was no need. His location was secure. Leaving was her only play. He knew part of her still believed in him, though.

"Lincoln," she yelled in every direction. "Come on! This isn't you! This isn't what Ruth would want. You have to see that. Lincoln!"

Morgan wasn't wrong. Ruth would never have understood. She would have tried though. Morgan, however, was lost to him. After a few more minutes of searching, he watched her vacate the junkyard.

He was alone. Truly alone.

He let more time pass, the cold a punishing blanket. Once he was satisfied his position remained secure, Lincoln shuffled loose of the Charger's backseat, rifle in hand. He watched Morgan's sedan blitz into the darkness. What else could she have done? While she had found the entrance to the yard he provided for her, it was far from the only one. Preparation meant multiple exit strategies. If he wanted to be followed he could have let her. But after hearing her anger, her inability to see the Witness' side of events, Lincoln required space. He needed time to think and plan for the next move.

Part of him wanted to scream out to her to apologize—to make it right. However, there were no more words for them. Their time together was done. It embittered him. Her reaction, unfortunately, had cemented the surety of his actions in Des Moines. He reached for the small note card in his pocket and held in before his weary eyes. The warning given to him by the man called the Witness. It was further proof he had made the correct choice at the time. The only one left to him.

He knew, Morgan. Even this, he knew.

The card beamed under the dawn, the small snippet a window into the answers held by the mystery man known only as the Witness.

Don't tell Agent Dunleavy the truth.

He should have listened. Part of him wondered if there was still time to make the right choice. Maybe it was too late. Maybe everything was as lost as he was.

CHAPTER TWENTY-EIGHT

The sun shone a little brighter that morning, and the air felt a little warmer. The shift caused puddles to pool from the snowbanks piled high along the Bethesda streets. Ben exited the police station, covering his eyes and holding tight to his hastily bandaged torso. His neck ached from the bruises that ran down to his shoulders. His legs were lead weights, his hands raw from the struggle with the specter. On top of everything was the lack of sleep from the previous two nights. The clock tower across the lane mocked him as it edged toward midday.

None of it mattered to him. None of it stalled his momentum or his resolve. He had survived, facing the nightmares of his youth instead of hiding under the blanket and hoping for the best. Ben had weathered the crisis and carried the wounds from it, to be sure. Beyond that, though, he'd had success in battling back the terror and fear dogging his steps for so long.

The case was closed—the death of Abigail Winslow, the woman once known as Abigail Hunt, was solved. Not an open-and-shut affair, not to him or anyone with a questioning view of the events, but Megan Daniels had taken care of the details with her confession.

The act surprised Detective Rutnall, but eagerness won out over concern at the ease of the solution. Ben sat in the corner, letting the pale woman explain the bitter revenge she had inflicted on Winslow. Some of the minutia was lost, and Cal's involvement at the scene never made it on the printed page. The same held true of the role played by Steven in the drama. Megan claimed full responsibility for the murder.

Rutnall asked few questions, both to the grieving Mrs. Daniels and to the waiting DSA agent who stayed at the Daniels home until the portly detective came to collect both of them. Cal had taken his rental car right after the visage of Steven Daniels left the premises, and Ben had been more than happy to keep him clear of the entire affair.

Ben hated leaving anything out. He disliked the idea of hiding the truth behind Winslow's death and how the case had changed his view of the afterlife. He, however, recognized the necessity behind the decision. Even Megan realized it would play better for her. A prison sentence for murder held more benefits than a lifetime in a mental facility upstate wearing a straitjacket and subsisting on anti-psychotics.

Ben was happy to have it behind him, happier still to be able to live to see another day. Steven had been freed of his obligation to his betrayed wife. Ben hoped his spirit might finally achieve some form of rest.

The morning was crisp and clear, but his next move was muddied and blurred with doubt. Work continued to call, demanding answers over his absence. Both Sullivan and Metcalf chimed in. His time was running out with them. Avoiding the subject was an impossibility. Additionally, avoiding the situation failed to solve anything. Confronting them and tackling the case stood as the only way to proceed.

The Grissom File still required processing, but only as a first step. He still believed his answers led back to what had happened to him in Buffalo and possibly the truth behind Emily Wright's disappearance. Doubts and growing darkness waited around every turn. Somehow, though, through the wisdom of a friend Ben noted the light balanced against all else. He planned to embrace that hope as long as possible.

He wanted to see things through to the end—just as his father would have done.

His worry fell away when a familiar sedan pulled to the curb across the street from the station house. Cal stepped into the sunlight, a nicely pressed navy-blue suit jacket over a new pair of khakis. His chestnut hair fell to the right in a large mess. His lower lip swelled from the punch taken from the desperate widow. The young attorney strode confidently toward the station, but stopped at the sight of the agent before the door.

"Look at this," Ben called with a smile. He slowly took the

steps to meet his new friend. People filtered around them, oblivious to their presence in the middle of the sidewalk. "If it isn't Cavlin Cooper, Attorney at Law."

Cal grinned, lifting his arm and the case at his side. "Briefcase and everything."

"I'm surprised to see you here," Ben admitted. "Had the feeling you'd be on your way home."

"I figured Megan could use some help after everything."

"Seriously?" Ben asked in surprise. He turned to the precinct, then back to Cal, who rocked casually along his heels. "You're going to —"

"Not me." Cal shook his head. "Not completely, anyway. I have a colleague in the area. Thought I would make the introductions."

Ben leaned close. "You do remember she tried to kill us, right?"

Cal ran a finger along his swollen lip. The sadness from the previous night returned to his eyes. "Out of grief. Loss. We both know what that can do."

Ben patted the man's shoulder. "You're a better man than me."

"I dress sharper too," he replied. "What's next for you?"

"Work. Unfortunately."

"Still worried about making the right decision?" Cal asked the distant agent.

"Yeah," he said with a smirk. "But it doesn't feel as big as it did a couple days ago. You? You going to keep using your gift?"

"Helping give Steven Daniels his well-deserved rest was the right thing to do," Cal said. He closed his eyes and let out a deep breath. When they opened again, they were wide and bright. "The dead need someone to speak for them."

"And your family?"

"I've spent the last year looking for answers for my own sake. It's time I started looking for theirs."

"I'm glad to hear it," Ben said. He extended his hand. "You let me know if you need anything, all right?"

Cal took his hand and gave it a stern shake. "Definitely."

"It was good to meet you, Cal Cooper."

"You too, Ben Riley."

Ben grinned and started down the street, his step lighter than it had been all morning. He heard Cal call to him from the base of the steps to the precinct, but he never turned. He didn't have to, as his friend said, "Good luck."

He simply waved his hand over his head, his words echoing in the morning light. "To us both, buddy."

Cal would be fine on his own. On some level Ben knew that even *he* would be fine. They had found a connection during their time together. Their kinship would last through the trials ahead, which made it easier to keep walking. He continued toward work, despite the pain of his injuries and the doubt at each deci-sion waiting for him. He kept moving ahead—a little lighter and a little brighter.

Good luck to us both.

CHAPTER TWENTY-NINE

She found him at the corner of Broad and Vermont. Ben shuf-fled down the block, his lips upturned in an ever-present grin. God, she hated that grin.

Morgan wiped the hair from her face, tucking it into place before wrapping a rubber band around the back. Reaching over to the passenger seat, she found her black Adidas ball cap and slipped her hair through the hole in the back. Leather gloves clung to her frozen fingers. She was tired of winter, even more tired of the day she had lost without a thing to show for it. The wind slammed into her as she left the warmth of the Impala. She fought through it, skirting across two lanes of mingling traffic and splashing through puddles to chase down her wandering colleague.

"Riley!" she called at the edge of the sidewalk. Ben stopped near a closed deli, his hand brushing the brick exterior for sup-port.

He turned, the smile fixed in place. How he managed it remained a mystery. He had an optimism that refused to quit no matter the circumstances. Was he merely naive to the world around him? Did he hide from that world with each grin? Or did the problem lie with everyone else?

"You came."

"You called," she said, annoyed. With barely three hours' sleep, most of which had come with clenched teeth and balled-up fists, she struggled to get moving. The trek to work had been a basket full of fun with blaring car horns and stop-and-go traffic for eight continuous blocks before Ben's call arrived. His voice was muffled compared to the louder ones in the background.

She recognized a police station when she heard one. Focusing on only Ben through the receiver, she'd noted his request on where to meet. With work scant minutes away she had turned toward the precinct across town, only to find Ben wandering the roads.

Annoyance faded behind concern at the sight of his face in full. Bruises ran down his neck, cuts were visible on his cheek, and the hand holding tight to the wall did so like a claw in the mortar, not the casual grip of a man hesitant about heading into work.

She moved for his side. "What the hell happened to you?"

"I fell down some stairs." He pulled back at her touch. She removed his hand from his left side and replaced it with her own. He nearly fell at the sensation and gently slid her hand away. He smirked through clenched teeth and bottled agony. "I'm fine, Morgan."

"You called me all the way here to tell me you're fine?"

He tilted his head to the Impala across the street. "I needed a…" His eyes fell on her. "Is everything all right?"

Morgan wondered how bad she appeared to cause his reaction. She had done her best to cover up the effects of the flash grenade with some makeup, but nothing could hide the effect the previous night had on her.

"Bad night."

"I miss something?" Ben asked, pressing the issue. "Looks like you pulled an all-nighter."

She held her tongue, surprised at the deflection. She was also surprised that he was the first person to reach out to her. Before her three hours of disastrous sleep, she had called Zac. It was late enough in the morning to pass off as work, and she'd needed someone to talk to before heading into Metcalf's office for a debriefing. Lincoln had hurt her in ways she didn't think possible by anyone other than her brother. She had never realized how close they had become until it had been yanked away like a security blanket deemed too childish.

Lincoln's friendship mattered. They had witnessed things together no one else would ever believe. They had helped unravel incredible mysteries. His betrayal had sent her head spinning. Questions nagged her about everything.

So she had reached out to the only person her mind allowed her to call — the only one closer to her than Lincoln. The man she had pulled to her bed less than forty-eight hours earlier. Zac had been distant on the line, distracted—though he refused to say about what. Hell, he'd refused to say Morgan's name during the call, which had given her pause. Then she'd heard *her* voice in the background: Claire Modine—Zac's wife. She had sounded bright and cheerful, even at such an early hour. Zac had ended the call quickly, a lie about paperwork lost at the office adding to her misery. Suddenly their perfect night together, an event she wanted to repeat, had crumbled before her eyes.

Zac hid in his marriage. Lincoln did the same in his false beliefs. There wasn't another option left to her. Yet Ben was here. He wanted to know about her long night and she held it back, brushed the pain of her failure aside with a shrug. "I doubt sleep would have helped."

"I hate that," he chided, seeing right through her denial.

"Care to share your night?"

He rolled his eyes. "Oh, it was a whole thing."

"Stop," she snapped and moved to his side. She helped him off the wall by taking some of his weight.

"Stop what?" he asked in jest. She threw him a hard glance.

"I'm not understanding your grin, Riley." Her hand rested on his chest. When he winced at the small amount of pressure placed there she shifted the hand to his side. "Bruised or broken?"

"Don't know."

"Yeah. Sounds like a fantastic day."

At the corner he turned to her, though Morgan kept her eyes on the traffic passing by. "Better than some. Yours went the other way?"

"Real quick." When the road cleared they shuffled across the street in unison. Ben's breathing was rapid even at their slow pace. When they reached the black sedan, she leaned him against the passenger side. "Listen..."

"Hey." He stopped her with a wave. "Partners, remember?"

She huffed. Even in pain he pushed her, pushed the relationship. She didn't understand why. The passenger door opened with a loud click before she circled the car. Her shoes quickly soaked through in the puddle growing along the gutter. "It's nothing you can help with. Trust me."

"Doesn't mean I can't try, right?"

Morgan hesitated. Ruth and Grissom were dead. Lincoln was lost, and his betrayal was a stinging wound in her heart. Zac remained a ball of question marks she couldn't unravel. At that moment, however, there was no mistaking who Ben Riley was to her: someone who wanted to listen.

Slowly she nodded. "Sure."

"Good," he said, slapping the hood of the car lightly. "Coffee run?"

She grinned. "You buying?"

"Only if you're driving."

She reached for the driver's-side door. "Definitely learning, Riley."

Both settled into the Impala and the engine came to life. Ben leaned deep into the seat. Each movement caused his smile to fade into a wince. He turned to her, and his two sympathetically exhausted brown eyes caught her own. "Morgan?"

"Don't tell me," she said with a sigh. "The hospital?"

"Oh yeah," he replied. "A hospital sounds real nice right now."

CHAPTER THIRTY

He should have told him the truth. The recrimination amplified as he stood under the bright light of the late-morning sun. The December wind blew his moppy hair in his face and he brushed it aside to keep the departing agent in view.

Cal couldn't take his eyes off Ben's staggered step, the strained gait carrying him farther down the road and deeper into Bethesda. Their night with the specter had taken more out of him than he cared to admit.

He was glad to have met Ben, gladder still to call him friend from the experience. If anyone else had busted into that apartment and found him over the dead body of Abigail Winslow, Cal held little doubt *he* would be the one seeking legal representation or worse.

Instead the pair had bonded, two lost souls trying to find their way in the world. They both sought to bring a little light back to the sea of darkness that seemed to surround them.

Clarity had come from the experience. Cal's gifts troubled him less, and the burden of interacting with the dead faded. The feeling had built over time, even before the loss of his family, yet he ran from it; he feared the repercussions of stepping too deeply into the world of the afterlife. Ben, however, was right. Cal had a talent—one that could do good for those in need. Keeping his gift hidden, running from the truth about what had happened to his family was no longer the answer.

That made it even harder to watch Ben depart, Cal knowing he hid the truth from a man desperate to trust someone. If only Ben hadn't asked the question. But the observant agent had noticed the presence on some instinctual level. Most did, though they were unsure what the sensation related to or what that chill in the air meant in a heated space.

The impression of someone or something in the room.

He asked, and Cal had denied it, playing the idea off as the joke he believed the burdened agent wanted to hear. Bringing pain and confusion to those around him was difficult to bear. It was his curse thanks to what he viewed from the other side. Ben had struggled with the gift, with the case in general. Cal understood that and accepted his hesitance. It wasn't until he had witnessed the arrival of Steven Daniels hovering above his wife that Ben had truly accepted Cal's point of view of the world.

Would he accept more? Would he want to know about the shadow following him down the road? Ben's burden ran deep. He needed to find his own path, not be set upon a new one thanks to Cal's admission. Being stuck in the past was a sure way to never face the future. It kept Cal from actively pursuing his family's death and was why he refused to set foot in the crime scene and see those he loved most in the world.

It wasn't Cal's decision to make here though. Cal should have told Ben the truth. Deep down it was the right thing to do. And yet, he didn't tell Ben about the man at his side, the one following his every move since they'd met in Winslow's apartment two nights earlier.

Ben's father.

Where most spirits relayed vital information or concerns to Cal, hoping to be heard one last time before moving to the next step, the wispy figure had uttered the same phrase repeatedly to his son. Two words whispered on the wind, lost to secrecy, yet no doubt echoing somewhere in the unconscious thoughts of Ben Riley.

I'm sorry.

ABOUT THE AUTHOR

Lou Paduano is the author of the Greystone series of urban fantasy adventures, which follow Detective Greg Loren and Soriya Greystone as they hunt myths, monsters, and legends in the city of Portents.

He is also the author of the conspiracy thriller series, The DSA, a serialized tale about a clandestine government agency trying to discover the true power behind humanity's future.

He lives in Grand Island, New York with his wife and three daughters. Sign up for his e-mail list for free content as well as updates on future releases at loupaduano.com.

CAL COOPER'S STORY
IS JUST BEGINNING…

The Cooper Massacre changed Cal's life forever. The secrets behind the death of his family are only the start of events that impact both sides of the veil.

The truths kept hidden by the Cooper family threaten to shatter Cal's faith, not only in those he lost but in everything he has ever believed.

See Cal take on the role of advocate to help solve crimes both in and out of the courtroom as he chases down the real demons of the world in an effort to find meaning of his life and the gift granted him.

The sharing of Cal's story lies in your hands. Email lou@loupaduano.com to tell me you want more. Only with enough reader responses will future *Spectral Advocate* stories come to light.

ALSO AVAILABLE NOW

It's her first case and it might be her last.

Soriya has worked her entire life to become the Greystone—protector of her city, Portents, against the growing shadows of myth and legend. All her efforts are in jeopardy when she is struck down by the destructive power of the Minotaur.

Soriya must now find a new path. Only one thing is certain—she's going to need help.

The secrets of Soriya's training are revealed in the first adventure of this new Greystone trilogy.

THE DSA CONTINUES IN…

A deadly virus is turning average people into killers.

Caught in the middle of the growing power struggle of the DSA, Ben Riley and Morgan Dunleavy are dispatched to solve the case in Buffalo — Ben's hometown and the place he was framed for murder.

Split between a need for answers to his past and an obligation to justice in the present, Ben winds up in the crosshairs of the madman behind the virus.

A madman everyone thought was dead.

Now Morgan must discover a cure to save Ben's life before it's too late.